RED ASSAUL

Also by Leo Kessler

THE IRON FIST
THE TRAITORS
WOLF

SS PANZER BATTALION
DEATH'S HEAD
CLAWS OF STEEL
GUNS AT CASSINO
THE DEVIL'S SHIELD
HAMMER OF THE GODS
FORCED MARCH
BLOOD AND ICE
THE SAND PANTHERS
COUNTER-ATTACK
PANZER HUNT

In the *Black Cossacks* Series:

THE BLACK COSSACKS
THE BLACK COSSACKS 2: SABRES OF THE REICH
THE BLACK COSSACKS 3: MOUNTAIN OF SKULLS

In the *Stormtroop* Series:

STORMTROOP
BLOOD MOUNTAIN
VALLEY OF THE ASSASSINS

In the *Rommel* Series:

GHOST DIVISION

In the *Foreign Legion* Series:

HELLFIRE

Leo Kessler

Red Assault

Futura Publications Limited
A Futura Book

A Futura Book
First published in Great Britain by
Futura Publications Limited in 1979

ISBN 0 7088 1601 0
Printed in Great Britain by
Hazell Watson & Viney Ltd
Aylesbury, Bucks

Futura Publications Limited
110 Warner Road
Camberwell, London SE5

DEATH VALLEY

'There is no adventure in heads-or-tails, in betting that the toss will come out life or death. War is not an adventure. It is a disease. It is like typhus.'

Antoine de Saint-Exupery

PROLOGUE

PROLOGUE

Brr . . . brr . . . brr . . .

The high-pitched scream of a Schmeisser machine-pistol split the icy January night. Tracer zipped through the sky. Glass shattered. A man screamed shrilly in agony as the remote village came to life. In spite of the enforced black-out, lights began to flash on everywhere, and cries and orders could be heard in Serbian and Croatian. As a slow British Bren gun started to hammer away, half-dressed, bearded men began to tumble out of the little thatched houses, struggling into their clothes and grabbing for their weapons at the same time. The attack on the partisan stronghold of Jajce had commenced.

'*Hurrah!*' the desperadoes of the 7th SS Volunteer Division *Prinz Eugen* cried hoarsely as they doubled forward across the frozen snow. '*Hurrah!*' They knew that they had caught the hated partisans of the 1st Proletarian Division completely off guard.

They plunged into the narrow streets, lit by the violent scarlet of small arms fire, crushing all opposition in front of them as they headed for the centre where the man they had sought for so long was known to be quartered.

A group of partisans under the leadership of a black-bearded under-lieutenant set up a machine-gun in a shop window, desperately attempting to hold up the bold attack. But they didn't last long. Grinning, a daredevil SS man, with socks wrapped around his boots to prevent him from slipping on the frozen snow, scrambled up the nearest drainpipe and onto the shop's flat roof. Leaning over, his teeth gleaming in the darkness, he dropped a bundle of six grenades down the chimney, crying, 'try that on for size, you Slav apes!'

There was a muffled *crump*, and then the roof began to heave and sway beneath his feet. The buckled machine-gun and half its crew flew out of the shattered window in a confused mess of flames and shattered limbs.

The *Prinz Eugen* men pressed home their attack. The partisans could not hold them back. Here and there, the men with the red star of the National Liberation Army on their fur caps started to raise their hands in surrender. But the SS desperadoes had been too long in the mountains of Jugoslavia to play that kind of game. The partisans would get a burst of fire in the guts or, if they were lucky, a brass rifle butt smashed into their faces. That was all they could hope for.

The heart had gone out of the partisan defence. They started to throw away their weapons and flee as their officers bellowed after them in red-faced anger. NCOs tried to bar their flight but were swept away in the panic. The division had broken.

The SS were already breaking into the little houses, booting out the old crones and the frightened, screaming children; pouring the fiery local plum brandy down their parched throats and letting the overflow run down their unshaven chins; grabbing the half-naked women and thrusting them onto the straw pallets, oblivious of their screams for mercy; and smashing incendiary grenades against the walls. The ambushes, the murders, the mutilations they had suffered at the hands of the partisans for the past two years in the mountains had hardened them. They had learned to expect no quarter and now would give none. Soon the village was ablaze.

Attila, the *Hauptsturmbannführer,* who had a wolfish face and an empty eye socket covered with a black patch, pulled the cheroot out from between his thin, cruel lips and took another swig from the bottle he held in his other hand. Then he looked down at the trembling official who knelt before him in the snow; his bodyguard's rifle muzzle held at the base of the man's shaven skull kept him still. 'All right,' he snapped, businesslike now, knowing that they did not have much time before the partisans rallied and counter-attacked. 'Where is he?'

The Serb quavered, 'Who, Mr Colonel?'

Attila put the end of his cigar against the official's left

hand and pressed hard. The Serb let out a piercing scream. Attila laughed harshly; it always gave him pleasure to inflict pain.

'I'm not a colonel,' he barked in fluent Serbian, 'and you know who I mean. We know that this dump Jajce has been the Red shit's HQ for the last two months. *Where is Tito?*'

'I don't know, sir! Honestly, I don't know!' the fat Serb cried piteously, his heavy jowls wobbling as tears poured down his ashen cheeks. 'He went . . . went away over a week ago now. Please . . . please, spare me!'

Attila spat out his cigar in disgust He knew the fat official was not lying. He was telling the truth all right; he was too scared for his life to do anything else. How often had they raided these God-forsaken mountain villages in the past twelve months, hoping to capture the elusive partisan leader, whose very name they did not really know, only to find that the cunning bastard had already flown. He nodded to his bodyguard grimly.

The German peasant boy, a native of Northern Jugoslavia who hated the Slavs with a passion, grinned in anticipation. He had carried out this part of his duties often enough in the past year; he even took pleasure from doing it neatly and efficiently, just as he had done when his father had asked him to slaughter one of the pigs on the farm.

'Watch your boots, sir,' he hissed and then pressed the trigger.

Crack! The back of the fat man's head burst like the shell of an egg. Blood and gore splattered the officer's mountain boots, but Attila did not care. He had failed once again and his mind was tormented by one overwhelming question: *WHERE WAS TITO?*

ONE: A MISSION IS PROPOSED

ONE

'*Meine Herren!*' Hitler commanded, stepping in the wood-panelled map room of the Wolf's Lair, followed by his alsatian bitch, Blondi.

Freiherr von Weichs, the Commander of Army Group South-West, and his subordinate, General Rendulic, Commander of the 2nd Panzer Army, stiffened to attention. '*Mein Führer*,' they barked in unison.

Hitler was unusually businesslike this morning. He was usually asleep at this time of the day, but today he had summoned the two generals from their HQ in Belgrade in his special plane and obviously had been waiting for them ever since the plane's touchdown at the nearby military field had been reported. 'Well?' he demanded.

Von Weichs looked at his subordinate.

Rendulic, an Austrian like Hitler, shrugged slightly, as if to say, 'All right, I'll take the blame then,' but he actually said, '*Mein Führer*, I'm afraid the operation was a failure. My men captured the village, but the bird had already flown. The gentlemen of the SS arrived a little too late.' His craggy, wrinkled face flushed angrily. 'For a year now we have been on this stupid merry-go-round and every time we have jumped off when the music has stopped, Tito's place has been empty!'

Hitler smiled coldly, but the outburst his officers had expected did not come. Instead he patted the side of the overly fat dog and said, 'Gentlemen, I didn't ask you to come here today to give you a lecture. But let me tell you something first about this chap Tito. We didn't take him seriously when he made his appearance in 1941. After all, what was he? An ex-sergeant, a smith and a jailbird, according to our intelligence sources. Besides, what did a few communist partisans matter in that crazy country, with right fighting left, Serb fighting Croat, Muslim against Christian, Catholic fighting Greek Orthodox? Divide and conquer was our motto. Let that pack fight among themselves – they wouldn't give us any trouble that way.' Hitler drew a breath, while the two generals waited, wondering if they were going to be treated to one of the Führer's hour-long lectures after all.

'All that changed in 1943 when our dear Italian allies surrendered to the enemy –' Hitler's voice was suddenly full of the Austrian's typical contempt for his Italian neighbours – 'and they conveniently arranged to place all their heavy weapons in Tito's hands. Suddenly, his bunch of ragged snipers were transformed into a real army, armed with heavy artillery, tanks and the like. Then those hypocrites, the British, switched their support from the conservative, royalist Chetnik partisans to Tito. For months now, they and the Americans have been parachuting arms and supplies in to him. All this has had its effect. Tito has been gaining recruits for his so-called National Liberation Army from all six Jugoslav nationalities – from men who are not communists. Today the Jugoslavs, with a few exceptions, gentlemen, are no longer fighting among themselves as they did in 1941 – now they are fighting against *us*!' He glared suddenly at the two silent generals, as if he were making them personally responsible for Tito's success in uniting his people in their fight against German occupancy.

The generals shuffled their feet uneasily and waited. For a moment or two, there was silence in the map room, broken only by the heavy breathing of the overfed bitch and the harsh crunch of the sentries' boots on the frozen snow outside.

'So what have we done so far,' Hitler continued with a barely suppressed sigh, 'apart from the usual abortive sweeps? Well, your predecessors in the Balkans, gentlemen, have had plans enough. That is certain. They have worked together with the Chetniks in an attempt to capture Tito by treachery. They have dropped dead bodies by parachute dressed in British uniforms with personal letters from that drunken sot Churchill to Tito hidden in their uniforms, triggered to explode when he opened them. They hired a traitor to poison his soup – or whatever the damned man's favourite food is. Once the man had his gold, they never saw him again . . .' He broke off suddenly. 'A hundred different schemes have been tried. All have failed. But even if we did manage to kill Tito, the cold-blooded British hypocrites would probably return their support to General Mihailovic's Chetnik's once again so that we would never be able to bring peace to that damned country. No, gentlemen, we must rethink our strategy in Jugoslavia.'

'What do you suggest, *mein Führer*?' Rendulic asked boldly, hoping to bring the lecture to an end, knowing that his fellow Austrian would excuse the interruption.

Hitler's dark eyes narrowed cunningly. 'We do not *kill* him – we *capture* him instead so that the whole partisan movement of our dear Marshal, as Stalin has pleased to promote him recently, is left in disarray. Leaderless and disorganized, they will revert to factions; it will take them months – and the British, too – to establish a cohesive resistance against us. By that time my wonder weapons will have won the war for us.' He patted Blondi fondly at the thought.

'How exactly do you wish us to capture Marshal Tito?' von Weichs, the sneer obvious in his voice, rasped in his supercilious Prussian manner. 'The man has his spies everywhere. As soon as we start to move troops out they start reporting by radio to Tito's HQ, wherever in three devils' name that might be at this moment!'

'Ah,' Hitler said, tapping the side of his nose knowingly, 'that is because you have been moving your troops *by land*. This time we'll move them *by air* – and even if that movement is spotted and reported in time, it will not matter, for we will already have our Trojan Horse inside the enemy camp.'

Freiherr von Weichs was caught off guard. His tight little mouth dropped open stupidly. 'Trojan Horse, *mein Führer*?' he gasped.

'Yes. For the surprise air attack will only be a gigantic

feint. The real job of kidnapping Tito will be carried out by a special formation of which you Rendulic, as an Austrian, might have already heard, for its members are mostly recruited in your Fatherland and Bavaria.'

Rendulic ventured a guess. 'Stormtroop Edelweiss of the High Alpine Corps?'

Hitler nodded. 'Exactly, the cream of the *Reich*'s mountaineers – Stormtroop Edelweiss, which I can reveal to you now, gentlemen, is already training hard for its vital mission.'

Hitler strode over to the big map of the Balkans which decorated one wall of the wooden hut. 'Now, gentlemen, let me tell you my plan for dealing with Tito once and for all...'

TWO

'Look at 'em, just look at 'em, will yer,' Ox-Jo, Stormtroop Edelweiss's sergeant-major, said in disgust, rubbing the back of his big cropped head. 'Idiots, the whole lot of them! The products of one thousand years of Germanic incest!'

Jap, his wizened, half-breed running mate, the result of a brief liaison between the daughter of a Bavarian technician on the German-American reconnaissance of Nanga Parbat in 1920 and an amorous Hunza guide-porter, nodded his agreement morosely. Together the two soldiers stared round the pathetically bare kitchen of the mountain farm, whose sole decoration was a hand-carved crucifix, lit by a flaring kerosene lamp.

At the scrubbed wooden table, an adenoidal boy with slack, dripping lips was banging away at the rock-hard flat bread of the mountains, trying to break it so that he could dip it in his ersatz coffee to soften it. Opposite him his teen-aged sister sat, with drooping breasts and bulging eyes, and stared at the two men with cretinous longing. At the green-tiled stove their mother, an enormous goitre bulging on the right side of her neck, was cooking a poor supper of boiled potatoes and milk curds.

'They've either got asses as big as half an acre, the women, or goitres as big as barrage balloons,' Ox-Jo Meier said miserably as he cleaned out the dirt of the day's field exercises from under his broken nails with a fork. 'You know, Jap, last night I tried to feel up one of these villages wenches and I was thinking I was doing a bit of good so I said to her, "Am I playing with yer tits all right?" in my usual charming manner. And she sez, "Those ain't my tits. That's my double goitre!"'

Jap laughed hollowly. 'Yer lucky yer can get a feel of a goitre,' he commented. 'All I've been feeling since we came up here in these shitting mountains is my peterman.'

'I never have time,' Ox-Jo said with a trace of his old humour and sighed. Outside it was snowing again; the flakes pelted against the cracked dirty panes like white flak.

'God, will we never get out of this dump!'

It was three weeks since the movement order had unexpectedly arrived at the Stormtroop's barracks in Graz. In the middle of the night, covered by the black-out, the hundred-odd men of Edelweiss had set out in a truck convoy, heading, according to their CO Colonel Stuermer, for the *Reich*. But they had not gone more than twenty kilometres when their lean, harshly handsome CO had ordered the convoy off the road into a snow-bound forest. Ten Fiat trucks, bearing the number plates of the new Fascist Militia, but driven by SS men, had been waiting for them. 'All right, men,' Stuermer had ordered, raising his voice above the howl of the wind, 'you'll find civvies in the backs of the trucks. Get changed at once. We've got a long journey in front of us. You can sort out the right sizes in boots when it gets light.'

Five minutes later, clad hurriedly in evil-smelling, second-hand clothes, they had been on their way again, heading south for the Austrian-Italian border.

Twenty-four hours later, again under the cover of darkness, they had halted at St Martin, a village in the Etschtal valley, part of the German-speaking Italian province of the South Tyrol. There they had taken the squeaking, rusty cable car up the mountain as far as it would go and had begun the fifty-degree ascent beyond. Weighed down with fifty kilos of equipment and weapons, and conscious of a sheer drop of 1,000 metres to the left of the narrow path, they had staggered, gasping, higher and higher, leaving the silver moonlit clouds far below them until they had finally reached the miserable collection of wooden houses and farms which clung to the steep side of the mountain wall. 'Vorra,' Colonel Stuermer had announced, the dawn sun tinting his sweat-lathered face blood-red. 'Stormtroop Edelweiss's new home.'

'*Home!*' had been Ox-Jo's exasperated comment, his breath fogging in the cold, thin mountain air. 'I've seen better outdoor shithouses!'

One day later Colonel Stuermer had disappeared and his second-in-command, Major Gottfried Greul, had taken over. In his usual arrogance, a soldier to his very fingertips despite the shabby civvies and his two-day-old blond beard, the Major had lectured them in the midst of a raging snow-storm, while the idiotic villagers had gawked at the sudden intruders from their windows.

'So you think you are civilians now, do you? Tucked away safely in this Alpine resort, remote from the war, eh? Well, you are wrong, very wrong.' He had eyed them fanatically. 'You are going to train like you have never trained before so that you'll be glad to go back to the front and have your stupid oafish turnips shot at by the enemy.' He had spun round and gestured through the flying white flakes. 'Somewhere up there two thousand metres above us is the Niederjoechl, leading into the Schnal valley. A good day's climb, you might think. Well, you are mistaken. Every day that dawns from now, you will climb it and return here *in the same day* – with fifty kilos of equipment on your shoulders. And you'll do it –' he had stared at them with gimlet-hard eyes – 'until you'll laugh and say, "Major Greul, can't we have something tougher to do?" *Dismiss!*'

And they had done just that, climbing day after day in some of the worst weather the South Tyrol had experienced in the last quarter of a century. Major Greul did not climb mountains as the CO did – because they were there was how Colonel Stuermer always attempted to explain his passion for climbing. He climbed the peaks to show to the 'decadent West' that a new star had appeared on the horizon – National Socialist Germany, young, vital and free from the sloth of Old Europe. Ever since the day in 1931 when he had conquered the north face of the Eiger as an eighteen-year-old Hitler Youth and had shocked the climbing world by planting the crooked cross banner on the summit, Greul had regarded climbing as a political act: every new conquest was a symbol of the new creed. Now without the restraint of Colonel Stuermer's presence, he forced the men of Edelweiss to newer and more strenuous efforts, driving them on with his tremendous, burning energy.

The Edelweiss troopers were all experienced climbers, tested in the Alps or Himalayas, or Bavarian or Austrian mountain boys, who had learned to climb and ski as children and had absorbed mountain lore with their mother's milk. But even these veterans could hardly stand the cracking pace that Major Greul set for them.

Each new day he had taken them up the Niederjoechl, regardless of the weather, finding a new route every morning, and increasing the difficulty of the climb rapidly: back-breaking pitches, calling for knee jams, presses-and-pushes, friction holds, with fifty kilos of equipment dragging at their backs, trying to force them from the rock-face so that their muscles had screamed under the pressure and their hearts had thumped in their rib-cages, as if they might burst out at any moment. Punishing chimneys, with the men scaling one hundred metre sheer rock-shafts, their bodies afire with pain, their shoulders raw where the rock had rubbed the flesh away, their breath coming in cruel, harsh gasps. Rope traverses that had even the boldest of them wide-eyed and trembling with fear as they swung back and forth over 500-metre drops, while their bleeding, broken-nailed fingers sought desperately for some kind of hold that would stop the frightening motion. And all the while, Major Greul punished his own iron-hard, lean body with almost religious intensity. He urged them on with contemptuous brutality, his arrogant voice ringing out over the mountainside with the cry that they had all come to hate: 'Tempo . . . *Tempo . . . What are you waiting for, you bunch of no-good weaklings . . . TEMPO!*'

'Heaven, arse and cloudburst!' a gasping Ox-Jo, with the

troop's 57mm mortar tube strapped to his enormous shoulders, had cursed more than once. 'What in God's name is he training us for – *an assault on Everest or something*?'

'But what is it all about and where's the CO?' Ox-Jo asked grumpily as they sat in the darkening kitchen, heaving his massive shoulder muscles to check if they were still functioning, his big broad bronzed face wrinkled with disgust as he watched the woman at the stove pick her nose with one hand while she stirred the wooden spoon in the curds for their supper with the other. 'Eh?' He emphasised his questions with a nudge to Jap's skinny ribs that nearly sent him flying from the wooden table.

'What do you think I do on Fridays? Walk across the water or something! How should I know,' Jap snapped, as tense as they all were after three punishing weeks in that remote mountain stronghold. 'All I know is I'll be glad to get out of this shitty village, back to somewhere where it's not as cold as an ice-bear's balls.'

'But I mean to say, you little yeller —'

'Eat!' the woman with the goitre cut in, slapping a great dollop of unappetizing curds on his cracked dirty plate and following it with a couple of potatoes, using her begrimed hand to take them out of the pan. 'Don't get good food like this down in the valley, you know.'

She repeated the performance with the others and then slumped down on her own chair, her weathered face suddenly wrinkled in a look of piety, her eyes tightly closed. 'Let us pray for what we are about to receive,' she whispered, crossing herself hastily.

'Let us pray indeed,' Ox-Jo echoed ruefully. 'Cos what we're gonna receive ain't gonna be any good. I can feel that in my bones – and I don't mean the grub.'

'Amen to that, Ox,' Jap agreed sombrely, picking up his fork.

Outside the snow storm raged, as if God on high wished to sweep this remote village off the face of the mountain and put an end to the plot that was being hatched there . . .

THREE

The slow-moving, three-engined Junkers 52 droned steadily over the snow-bedecked hills below, covering kilometre after kilometre of apparently empty countryside. Here and there there were little groups of straw-roofed white houses dotting the emptiness, but with no smoke coming from their chimneys. They had long been abandoned, and the rough country tracks scratched across the hillsides at impossible angles were devoid of life. The savage fighting of the past few years in Jugoslavia had emptied the countryside below of the peasants and small farmers. They might as well have been flying over the surface of the moon.

Colonel Stuermer yawned again and rubbed his weary eyes. He knew he was not required to go on these flights, which seemed to be routine *Luftwaffe* transport operations but were in reality a cover for something else. But they did give him a chance to study the terrain over which they would have to march – and perhaps have to fight. He felt out of place and useless in the slow transport's narrow fuselage, now crammed full of *Luftwaffe* radio detection experts with their ears glued to their earphones, trying to establish the direction from which came the radio messages sent from the elusive partisan leader's secret headquarters.

Twice they had intercepted messages which had caused the plane to buzz with excitement. But when decoded, they had turned out to be routine messages from the English SOE,* attached to partisan sub-units, to their headquarters in Greece. They had given no clue to the whereabout of Tito's HQ.

This day, however, they were flying a north to south course, from Banya-Luki to Split on the Dalmatian coast, right

* Special Operations Executive, a wartime British intelligence organization.

across the partisan-held area of Jugoslavia. They had flown over the dull-silver snake of the River Verbas, around Jajce, Tito's former HQ, and were now heading for Livno, which might be a likely place for him to have established his new stronghold.

In the middle of the slightly swaying fuselage, the bespectacled, clever, portly signals officer in charge, *Hauptmann* Wallny, tirelessly kept his eye on his signallers, who were constantly adjusting their delicate instruments, trying to get a fix. Stuermer sighed, wishing he were back with his men in the pure air of the high mountains and away from this swaying metallic cage which smelt of fuel, sweat and stale vomit. Would they never find the HQ?

Time passed leadenly. The plane's engine droned on. There was no sound save the steady throb of its motors and the soft buzz of morse. Stuermer closed his eyes. Bored and lazy, he started to drift off into sleep.

He awoke with a start. In the same instant that the plane shuddered, there came the slow rapping of flak on its metal frame. The tallest of the operators sprang up from his seat, crying excitedly, 'Captain . . . Captain, I've got it!'

'What, syphilis?' Wallny yelled, preventing himself from falling just in time as the pilot swung the plane suddenly into a steep bank to avoid the shells exploding outside.

'Something's coming through!'

Stuermer sat up. He flung a look at the operator, who started to scribble furiously on his pad, while outside the shells came closer and closer.

'Come on . . . come on, then,' Wallny cried, crouching over the operator, clicking his fingers nervously. 'Where . . . what? Hurry it up, man, or they'll have one right up our arse in a minute!'

The plane rocked violently as a shell exploded directly below it.

'Gentlemen,' the young pilot's voice came over the tannoy, controlled yet urgent, 'could I recommend a little more haste? I'll have to start taking evasive action soon –' the plane swayed alarmingly as a shell erupted to starboard, thrashing the frame with hissing shrapnel – 'or I'm afraid we'll be walking home.'

Wallny flashed Stuermer a look of anxiety.

The Colonel shook his head. 'Get that fix first, Captain,' he called above the roar of the guns. 'Then we'll break off!'

Sweat pouring down his forehead, the operator scribbled on while the plane shimmied back and forth. The fuselage filled with smoke. Great tears appeared dramatically in the metal skin. Aluminium debris soon lay everywhere on the floor. One operator screamed and then fell, gurgling blood. Still the listening operator kept writing down the vital message. Now the whole horizon seemed to be erupting in flame. They were flying ever deeper into a tremendous flak concentration. Even in this fearful moment, Stuermer knew that the number of guns being employed indicated that they were approaching a vital area. Was this it?

'Gentlemen, I am now crapping very thinly through the eye of a needle,' the pilot's voice came through the tannoy. 'If I could beg you *please* to get the digit out of your orifice and —'

'I've got it!' the operator screamed, springing to his feet and pulling off his sweaty earphones.

'Quick!' the Captain gasped.

'It's in Russian. What it says we'll have to leave for the experts to decode. But it's intended for the *Stavka* * PFX located at Drvar.'

'It's Tito's main HQ!' Captain Wallny cried triumphantly. 'The Ivan Military Mission, we know, is attached only to the main HQ. They're there to keep an eye on Comrade Tito —'

Stuermer did not wait to hear any more. 'In three devils' name,' he exclaimed, 'let's get the hell out of here while we've still got a whole skin.' He staggered up the littered, madly swaying gangway past the dying radio-man to where the sweating pilot, his face ashen now, clung grimly to the controls, the perspex of the cockpit in front of him a shattered spider's web of gleaming splinters. 'Get the shit out of here,

* Soviet High Command.

pilot. And don't forget our little trick.'

The pilot needed no urging. 'Thank God for that, sir,' he cried through gritted teeth. 'I've just peed through my parachute.'

He swung the ancient transport round in a low bank and pulled the toggle which activated the smoke dischargers attached to the two outer engines. At 300-kilometres per hour, the Junkers 52 started to plunge towards the low hills on the horizon, trailing two twin streams of ugly black smoke behind it, which indicated that is was heading for a crash.

Below, the young, excited gunners of the 2nd Proletarian Division dropped their shells near the breeches of the smoking guns and clapped each other on the shoulders. Caps were thrown into the air and hoarse cheering broke out. 'We've got the Fritz! . . . We've got the bastard!' they cried exuberantly.

Untouched by the excitement of his young gunners, the elderly, bespectacled under-lieutenant in charge followed the progress of the enemy plane to its doom with his binoculars. It dropped lower and lower, smoke streaming from its shattered engines. He could imagine the pilot fighting to lift it. Then the plane vanished behind the hills. There was a silent flash, followed moments later by a hollow boom, which resounded among the hills. Then silence.

Slowly, the elderly artilleryman lowered his glasses, with a smile of satisfaction on his face. Another Fritz spy plane had bought it.

FOUR

'Gentlemen, we of the radio detector service of the *Luftwaffe* are sure, *completely sure*, that Tito's HQ is located at Drvar.' Wallny, flushed and excited, began to wind up his report to the assembled officers, under the hard unyielding gaze of General Rendulic. 'My three land location stations – Vakuf in the north, Knin in the south-west and Srnetica in the east – have confirmed the original airborne reading. The volume of radio messages is too great for a sub-unit and it is the only place from which messages in Russian are coming. Drvar is the place.' He paused, gasping for breath.

Rendulic nodded. The Captain sat down, obviously pleased with himself. Stuermer smiled slightly at the little man's naïvety. For him it was all over. He had solved the mystery and that was that. But for the officers assembled in the big Belgrade briefing room the bloody business had just begun.

Rendulic turned to the nervous young lieutenant who represented the *Luftwaffe*'s photo-reconnaissance service. 'Photo-recon,' he snapped, as if it was the fresh-faced officer's name.

'Sir?' As he sprang forward, his papers and photos fell to the floor. But there was no laughter from the officers sitting around Stuermer. Their lean, tough faces, hardened by years of the most cruel fighting on all fronts, remained tense and unrevealing. Stuermer knew the faces of old. They were the faces of the best National Socialist Germany could offer in this fifth year of the great battle; they were men like himself, who knew that missing the slightest detail at a briefing like this might mean their own death and that of many good men under their command. They had no time for tit-sucking youths such as the embarrassed young Air Force officer here, who had still got egg-shell behind his ears.

'Well, gentlemen,' he began finally, throwing out his narrow chest, which was adorned solely with the Sports Medal in Bronze while his audience was laden with tin collars and all the rest of the cheap baubles with which the Third Reich rewarded bravery and the sacrifice of blood, 'Photo Recon has come up with this. To judge by vehicle tracks and radio masts, the HQ must be located here —' he indicated the spot on the blow-up – 'at a place we call the Citädel. However, Tito himself does not spend the night there. How do we know?' He beamed winningly at them, but his bright smile was not reflected in the hard faces of the old campaigners listening to him. 'I shall tell you. Three times our photo recon planes have spotted a jeep, accompanied by a very heavy escort – which can only indicate a very important personage – leaving just before darkness for this place here.' He tapped the second photo which he had managed to pin up with some difficulty. 'It's the remote mountain village of Batasi, some six kilometres from Drvar. And the jeep tracks, as you can see from photo number three, lead up to a cave or some sort of bunker on the sheer rock face – *there.*' He tapped the photo, as his listeners craned their necks to make out the details. 'Our conclusion at Photo Recon is that is where Marshal Tito spends his – hopefully – lonely nights.'

Rendulic glared at him from beneath his shaggy eyebrows and the young lieutenant sat down again hurriedly, without waiting for the usual questions, glad to be removed from the attention of those fierce eyes.

General Rendulic took the centre of the stage once more and barked, 'Briefing officers out – *please.*'

The *Luftwaffe* officers left quickly. They had played their role. Now it was up to the fighting men.

Rendulic waited until they had closed the door behind them and the sentry had locked it once more, then he said, 'You must realize, gentlemen, that the enemy has eyes everywhere. Previously we have failed in our operations against this chap Tito because we have never been able to achieve surprise. The enemy has always known what we were going to do in advance. This time it will be different. Captain Ryska, please.'

'Herr General!' The Commander of the 500th SS Parachute Battalion stamped to his feet and strode swiftly to the podium. He was a broad-shouldered, tough-looking man with his chest covered in decorations and a livid scar running down the left side of his head. 'My plan? As follows. Battalion drops in two phases. Red and Black.' He barked out his terse phrases, as if his narrow lips were working on steel springs. 'I take in Red. My second-in-command will lead Black. Black's objective will be to take Anglo-American and Russian liaison units. Radio station. Cut off communications with outer world. Understand?'

Hard-bitten veterans that they were, the officers nodded in agreement, as if they were raw recruits.

'Red will secure area round Citädel, their high command. As soon as gliders arrive —' he nodded in the direction of the paratroop officer from General Student's HQ * – 'we push on to the caves where he sleeps. That's all. Captain Attila.'

The veteran partisan-hunter with the black patch over one eye got to his feet and stubbed out his cheroot with elaborate slowness. He swaggered to the rostrum, his Knight's Cross tinkling softly, as did the silver spurs he affected on his highly polished riding boots even when he was not on active service. 'Thank you, Captain,' he said without meaning it. His one eye swept his listeners' faces cynically, contemptuously, as if he were not at all impressed by them and the accumulated tin of five years of war.

'Now the stubblehoppers come into the act,' he began. 'The hairy-assed, poor stubblehoppers. We break through to the gents who drop out of the blue and assist them to carry out their mission.' He pronounced the word 'assist' as if he had just said someone had made love to his grandmother.

Colonel Stuermer smiled. Captain Attila of the *Prinz Eugen* Division was a joker.

'Yes,' Captain Ryska burst in, full of the typical, brutal SS dash, which had given the Black Guards the highest number of casualties in the whole of the *Wehrmacht*. 'Together

* Head of the German Parachute Army.

we advance to the caves. Tito eliminated. Finished. Operation over. Successfully.' He glared at General Rendulic, as if daring him to disagree.

Rendulic knew better, although he was a full general and the scar-faced SS man was only a captain. 'Quite so, Captain,' he said tamely, 'quite so. So, gentlemen, that is all for now. The tentative date for the commencement of the operation is the first week of May. Some two weeks from now. I shall send you now on your various ways so that you can get on with your planning. But let me emphasize this once – secrecy, *absolute* secrecy, is vital.' He stiffened to attention. 'Gentlemen, thank you for coming.'

The assembled officers clicked to attention. Ryska thrust up his right arm woodenly and bellowed at the top of his voice, '*Heil Hitler!*'

Next to him one-eyed Captain Attila flipped up a limp wrist and echoed the words without enthusiasm.

Noisily chairs were thrust back, and as soon as the door was opened, the officers began to file out, past the heavily armed sentries everywhere. Puzzled and wondering why he had been summoned to this conference, Stuermer started to follow until Rendulic caught his eye. His lips formed the silent word '*Stay*'.

FIVE

'*Prost*, Stuermer!' Rendulic raised his glass of brandy. 'Damned fools those SS, but brave.' He downed the fiery spirit in one gulp, as if trying to wash away a bad taste.

'*Prost, Herr General!*' Stuermer echoed and followed suit, wondering why he in particular had been asked to stay behind. Outside the sound of the departing staff cars had died away and all was silent save for the stolid stamp of the sentries.

'You know, Stuermer, there are many important things involved in this operation which are not immediately apparent to simple soldiers like ourselves.'

Stuermer feigned polite interest, Rendulic was anything but a simple soldier. For an Austrian to become an army commander in the Greater German *Wehrmacht*, he had to be a politician.

'We have to show our allies in the Balkans, Rumania, Bulgaria and Hungary – as well as the neutrals, in particular Turkey – that we can cope with the enemy in our own backyard – Tito. And we have to achieve a cheap victory. We have neither the troops nor the resources to tackle his whole damned army. Somehow we must divide that rabble of southern Slavs long enough until we have gained a decisive victory at the Front. Then the Marshal's ramshackle empire will fall apart of its own accord. Thus, the Führer has ordered Tito must be *captured* but not *killed*.'

'Do the SS know that?' Stuermer asked, remembering the look on Captain Ryska's hard face.

'Oh, that brave idiot!' Rendulic dismissed him with a wave of his manicured hand. 'No, this is where you come in, my dear Stuermer. The Führer in his infinite wisdom has offered me the services of Stormtroop Edelweiss.'

Stuermer grinned. Rendulic was definitely *not* a simple

soldier. His contempt for the Great Captain of All Times, as the propaganda apparatus called Hitler, was obvious. 'Why us, sir?'

'Because our bold SS men think they are going to make the running. They aren't, Stuermer. You are. They are simply a diversion to occupy the partisan intelligence services. Willing bodies prepared to die for some desperate glory.' He shrugged eloquently. 'Fortunately, in this year 1944, Germany still possesses such silly, brave young men. Now then, Stuermer, here is what this operation is really about. I want you to take your Stormtroop and do this...'

When he had finished outlining his plan, the craggy-faced General refilled their glasses with cognac. He raised his own and hesitated momentarily, as if for the very first time he realized the full enormity of the task he had just given the mountaineer; then he barked, '*To success, Stuermer!*'

'*To success!*'

Their emptied glasses shattered in the great stone fireplace like the last bullets of a firing squad.

TWO: JOURNEY INTO THE INTERIOR

ONE

The Citädel shook again as the dive-bombers came in for another attack, their sirens screaming, the multiple flak hammering away at them. Next to his chair, Tiggan, trembled with fear. Tito bent down and patted the dog reassuringly and then put another English cigarette into the little pipe he smoked. Calmly, he listened to the excited conversation going on all around him in the map room, his broad Slav face half-concerned, half-amused.

All day long the Fritzes had been bombing Drvar. To him that indicated they knew the whereabouts of his new HQ, though the knowledge did not worry him particularly. Nor did it seem to worry his Chief-of-staff, Jovanovic, either. He stood in the middle of the excited staff officers, his intelligent face set and unmoved, as he attempted to pacify them.

'Comrades, even if these raids do mean they are going to attack us, they'll bite their teeth out on this position. Even without the three corps of the National Liberation Army, we can easily defend it. The position is virtually impregnable, and we know every goat-track into the mountains, every stone.' His voice rose confidently. 'Why, with a couple of men and a sturdy boy, we could defend these mountains against the whole German army!'

Tito waited until the howl of the dive-bombers and the crump of bombs passed, then he took his pipe out of his mouth and said, 'I agree with Comrade Jovanovic, but what, I ask myself, if this aerial softening-up is a prelude to a different type of Fritz attack?'

A dozen heads swung round to stare at him.

'Yes, comrades,' he continued, 'what if the Germans intend to drop paratroops on top of us?'

His words had an electric effect. A heated discussion broke out immediately. Arguments were tossed back and forth as

SITUATION IN YUGOSLAVIA MAY 1944

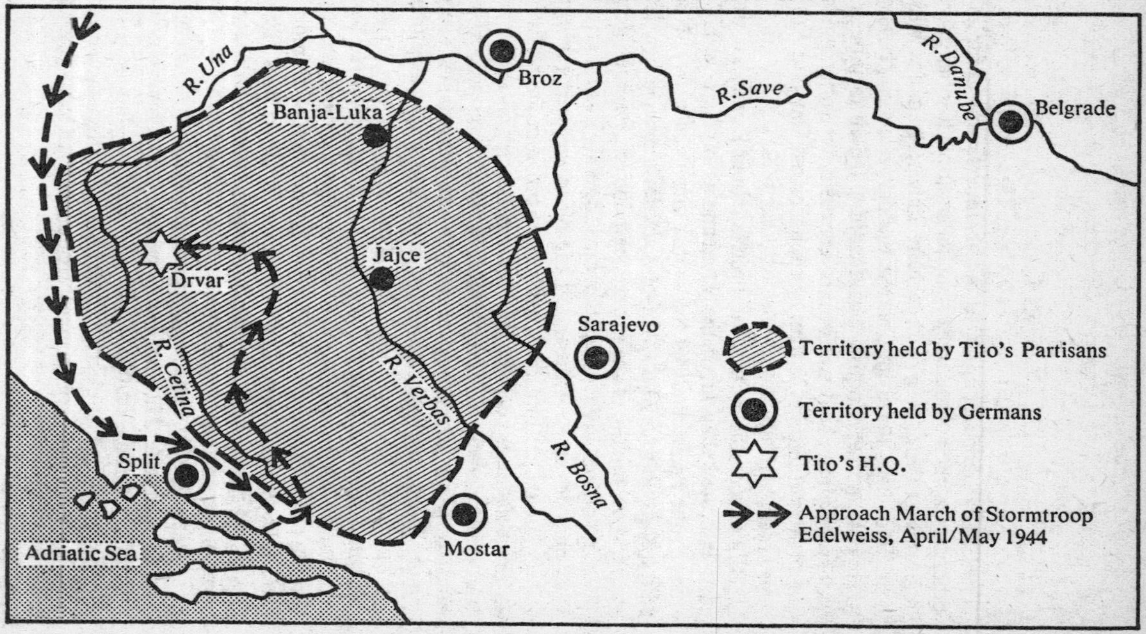

the German Stukas howled down once more, their machine-guns chattering like angry wood-peckers, the flak thumping away furiously. In the end the Chief-of-Staff raised his voice above the others and snapped authoritatively, 'All agents report, comrades, that there there are no German paratroops or gliderborne soldiers in the whole of the Balkans. As far as I can find out from the English mission here, the nearest Fritz para formations are in Northern Italy and Southern France. Apart from that, the Fritz paras have not risked a full-scale airborne attack on a seriously defended position since they tackled the English in Crete in '41. They had a bellyful there. They beat the English, but they broke their own backs doing so. My belief is that if they do attack they will do so by land. Aud thus far we have no indication from agents in Croatia or Serbia that they are preparing for a land attack.' He looked at the heavy-set, dark-haired man in the chair, who was stroking his trembling dog thoughtfully. 'Comrade?' he enquired.

'Probably you are right, Jovanovic,' Tito said slowly, his brow creased in a frown. 'Our positions here are very strong. But why these persistent air attacks? No, the Fritzes are up to something. I can feel that in my bones, but what it is I don't know.' His voice hardened. 'Whatever game they are playing, we must play it smarter. Your pad, Jovanovic.'

The block appeared in the Chief-of-Staff's hands, as if by magic. The perfect staff officer, he waited attentively, pencil poised, while Tito collected his thoughts.

'Two things. One. To all agents. Priority number one for all agents is to be on the look-out for German paratroops, gliders, any sign of their undertaking airborne operations. Ensure, Jovanovic, that all agents have details of the Fritz paratroop insignia so that they can recognize them.'

'It will be done, comrade.'

'Two. Special to Comrade Captain Popvic of the Eleventh Kozara Brigade.'

There were soft chuckles from the younger staff officers. They all knew the legendary Captain Popvic – one-time perfumed dandy, member of the Royal Guard and darling of

Belgrade's society women, who surprisingly had thrown in his lot with the communist partisans to become one of the National Liberation Army's most feared killers. Tito grinned, too, though a little voice deep inside him said, 'One day you'll have to have him shot, you know. But after we have beaten the Fritzes.'

'Herewith he is ordered to ensure that all German troop transports entering Jugoslavia from either Italy or Austria are to be destroyed. As from now, German reserves are not to enter the country under any circumstances. Understood, Jovanovic?'

'Yes, comrade.'

'Good.' Tito rose to his feet and the frightened dog began to wag its tail expectantly. 'I'm going back to the caves. The English are coming to eat tonight and you know how those capitalists can drink, especially that one with the skirt. I must hide my whisky.'

The staff officers laughed dutifully, knowing that Tito meant the head of the English Mission, who affected a kilt. Then they stamped to attention, hands raised to their foreheads in salute.

Marshal Tito acknowledged the salute and went out into the debris-littered street, where his jeep was already waiting for him. It was April 20th, 1944. He had exactly one more month to live.

TWO

Steadily the long, slow troop-train chugged up towards the mountain pass. At the front were two heavy locomotives, decorated with the white-painted slogan *Wheels Rolled for Victory.* In the event of a mined track, the first locomotive, which was empty, would be sacrificed. Then came the flak car, with the crew of the quadruple 20mm flak cannon made monstrous by the leather face masks they wore for protection against the icy air. Behind it came the long line of coaches, filled with returning leave-men and reinforcements. At the end of each coach, in a raised look-out tower, a freezing soldier searched each side of the track for any sign of the earth being disturbed. To the rear, just before the guard's van, was a long goods coach; usually it was filled with horses or heavy equipment, but this day it was occupied by scruffy unshaven civilians, who – the train commandant had been informed – were Jugoslavs working for the Ministry of War, hence their presence in a German troop-train.

In the middle of the train, known to be the safest place in case of an attack, there was the train commandant's coach, filled with communications equipment and a well-trained SS anti-partisan commando, which would spring into action at the first sign of trouble. Not that the one-armed, fat second-lieutenant who was the train commandant expected any trouble on this trip. At every five kilometres he telephoned ahead to the track commandant, usually a corporal who was responsible for ensuring that the next stretch of rail was free of mines and traps. Even if the partisans did manage to slip in after the corporal had checked his section, the pudding, as he called the first locomotive and the last coaches filled with third-class citizens, would bear the brunt of the attack. By the time the partisans had dealt with the pudding, the rest of the train would be alerted. Thus, as the train steamed up to the pass, the train commandant relaxed in his plush seat, his mind full of Irma, the strapping German with whom he would spend the next forty-eight hours in Belgrade, just as he had spent the last forty-eight with Mitzi, an equally strapping Austrian girl in Graz. A better bus conductor, he told himself happily, although this particular one was a lieutenant of the Greater German Army, who bore the German Cross in Gold on his breast and had one empty sleeve, a legacy of Moscow in '41.

He closed his eyes and thought pleasurably of what was waiting for him in Belgrade in ten hours' time.

'Do you know, Jap, if that tart in Graz had of worn a shorter skirt, she would have had to shave,' Ox-Jo was saying raising his voice above the bellows of the troopers playing skat at the other end of the long straw-filled coach.

'And if the dog hadn't have stopped to piss, 'Jap said apropos of nothing, 'he'd have caught the shitting rabbit.'

'But I tell you, chicken-shit, she had a muff right down to her fat knees,' Ox-Jo persisted, taking a bite at the end of his ration salami.

'Should have kept yer warm at least,' Jap said scornfully. 'That's about all yer good for with a tart, you big Bavarian barn-shitter, you.'

'That's about all I had time for in this mob. Yer just start getting 'em a bit on heat and you're back in the shitting train on yer way to God knows where.'

Jap looked out of the chink in the door at the snow-capped, desolate mountains. 'Yes, where do you think we're off to this time, Ox?'

Ox-Jo shrugged his massive shoulders. 'Search me. They give yer all the lung torpedoes yer want, real bean nigger-sweat and enough sauce to get me blue and you ask me what gives. Ain't you got all yer cups in yer cupboard, Jap? They're sending us off for the chop, that's what gives.'

'But they allus do,' Jap protested, staring around the coach, filled with snoring, bearded men, their Russian Tommy guns hanging from nails driven into the walls, next to their mountaineering equipment. 'But where and for what?'

Ox-Jo tapped the side of his big nose solemnly. 'That, my little hairy-assed friend, is a secret known only to the All-Highest, the Führer, and probably some constipated wet-tail of a lance-jack in the High Command. Now knock it off, I'm going to get some sack time in.' With that he took one last, disgusted bite at his sausage and rolled over, eyes closed, in the straw.

The problem of their destination and their assignment puzzled Major Greul, too, as he faced Colonel Stuermer at the end of the coach, seated on a ration case. Stuermer had been devilishly secretive when he had returned to the remote mountain village. After assembling them in a barn, with the wind howling outside like a banshee, he had said simply, 'We are going on a train ride to Belgrade. But, comrades, we will never arrive there.' That and no more.

Thereafter, there had been another mysterious midnight move, changing trains secretly at Bolzano, then Brenner, and again at Linz until they had finally boarded the troop-train at Graz. They had long crossed the Jugoslavian frontier at Ljubljana, and he was still as mystified as ever.

Major Greul removed his lips from the canteen of cold coffee, the likes of which he had not tasted in years and said, 'It all seems highly irregular, sir,' His tone was somewhat reproachful, as if he were offended by Stuermer's reticence.

'Why, Greul?'

'Well, I mean, sir, these dreadful civvies and travelling like this as if we were a bunch of East Workers.* And why have we been armed with Russian machine-pistols and climbing gear when our own German equipment is far superior?'

Stuermer took a sip of his own coffee, savouring the fra-

* The name given to imported labour from the occupied Eastern countries.

grance. 'My dear Greul, you will be told all in due course.'

'But I'm your second-in-command, sir. If anything should happen to you and I have to take over, I'd be completely lost. I have no idea of our destination or our mission.'

Stuermer sighed inwardly. He knew it was time to mention the heavy guns or he would have no peace for the rest of this long boring trip to Zagreb, where the train would make an unexpected stop. 'Greul,' he said, 'I'm sorry to have to be so heavy about this, but the Führer himself ordered the strictest security on a need-to-know basis. And at this juncture, you do not need to know our objective.'

The mention of the Führer's name did the trick. Greul was a fanatical National Socialist. His face hardened and his arrogant eyes gleamed. 'I understand completely, *Herr Oberst*,' he snapped and flushed down the rest of his coffee with a swagger. 'I'll go and check if that one-armed idiot of a train commandant is doing his job correctly. Discreetly, of course. That pass up ahead is a likely spot for an ambush.'

'That is a good idea, Greul,' Stuermer said. He waited until Greul had gone, then leaned his back against the swaying wooden wall and stared out at passing countryside. The blizzard had ceased and as they crawled up the pass towards a spidery, gleaming bridge, everything sparkled bright and white with the preternatural clarity of vision that always comes after a snowfall. The place did seem ideally suited for an ambush. Stuermer closed his eyes and forgot the danger, his mind already busy once more with the tremendous task ahead.

'Here they come, Comrade Captain!' the look-out hissed.

'Cover – on the double!' Captain Popvic ordered, stubbing out the gold-rimmed perfumed Balkan cigarette which he preferred to the para-dropped English ones.

Veterans all, his Kozara partisans ducked behind the cover of the snow-covered bushes on the mountainside, while Popvic observed the scene below from his hiding place.

The little group of German soldiers, middle-aged, fat, and huddled in greatcoats and scarves, were coming down the track now, their dogs straining at the leashes, sniffing the snow eagerly.

Popvic smiled and stroked his thin black moustache, which looked as if he pencilled it on every morning after shaving. The dogs would not find anything – here.

The alsatians had been trained to sniff out the TNT used in mines. But his men had taken the precaution of rubbing the opening in the mines from which the odour of TNT came with black marhoka tobacco to cover the smell of explosive. Two kilometres farther up the track, however, they had deposited small doses of loose TNT everywhere. That would drive the dogs wild, sending them digging for mines all over the place, and would keep the Fritzes busy for a while.

Popvic switched his amused gaze from the dog-handlers to the fat, helmeted corporal on the tired nag, which drooped under the weight while he surveyed the track ahead with his binoculars. He knew the German's task was to check the ground ahead of the dog to see if the surface had been disturbed since it had been raked that morning. But any footprints the Kozaras might have made had long been cleared away with their own rakes. No, Popvic told himself, the Fritzes would find nothing to make them suspicious this morning.

Five minutes later the track-corporal's party had passed on, having discovered nothing. Popvic grinned happily. This would make the twentieth train he had blown up since he had received the new order from Tito. He reached in his pocket and took out one of his gold-rimmed cigarettes. With a flourish of his gold-plated lighter, he lit it and contentedly exhaled a stream of blue smoke.

It was a careless move. Stuermer's keen gaze caught it immediately; a tiny spurt of blue-red flame, on the snow-covered mountainside to their right. Who was out there in this God-forsaken wilderness? The answer came in a flash.

'Ox!' he yelled, springing to his feet and grabbing for his Russian Tommy gun. 'Get the men —'

In that same moment, the series of electrically operated mines exploded under the two locomotives. The train bucked like a wild horse feeling the weight of a saddle for the very first time. The coaches concertina'd back and forth in a grinding slither of metal and protesting, splintering wood.

Behind the flak coach the next series of mines exploded underneath the stalled train, crashing into the stores car. A soldier screamed shrilly as he was pierced from back to front by a bottle of schnaps. Frozen cherries flew around like red tracer. The fat train-commandant, still dreaming of tits, was hit in the face by rock-hard frozen breast of chicken, and fell grievously wounded, his mouth full of chicken tit. The latrine at the rear of the coach erupted, drenching the dead and the dying with soaked newspaper, urine and faeces.

Crouched behind their cover on both sides of the shattered train, the partisans open up with their machine-guns. The illegal dum-dum bullets, which they had made themselves, slammed into the confused, panic-stricken men who were trying to escape from the overturned coaches, fighting each other to get out of the way of the scalding steam streaming from the wrecked locomotives. Men went down everywhere in the melting snow, screaming in agony as the dum-dums split open in the centre when they struck their targets, like lethal four-petalled flowers blossoming, ripping gaping holes in their victims.

Stuermer flung a hasty glance at the chaos in his own coach. No one had been hurt, but already the enemy's slugs were ripping out great chunks of wood from the coach-walls and sending them flying everywhere like angry brown hornets. It would not be long before Edelweiss started taking casualties.

Stuermer knew it was no use trying to get his men into the open; the enfilading fire would slaughter the troopers. They would be sitting ducks. '*Ox-Jo!*' '*Jap!*' he bellowed above the frantic crackle of small-arms fire. 'Follow me!'

Stuermer doubled back to the end of the wrecked coach, not bothering to check whether they were following him. He flung open the door and dropped to the tracks. Fifty metres away a dark, bearded face under a black fur cap loomed up. And another. Unhesitatingly Stuermer pressed the trigger of his machine-pistol.

The partisans crumpled and fell to the ground like discarded puppets. Another bearded giant rushed forward, brandishing a sabre. Behind Stuermer, Jap pulled the china pin out of a stick grenade and lobbed it. The giant disappeared in a ball of violet fire, his sabre flying high into the air with his severed, gloved hand still holding it.

Stuermer slung his Tommy gun over his shoulder, while Jap and Ox-Jo on the metal platform above looked down at him, ignoring the slugs whining everywhere. Further up the train the survivors were being systematically slaughtered by the partisan crossfire. Stuermer knew he could not save them; his first duty was to his own men.

He bent and grabbed the icy coupling. With all the strength in his lean but muscular body, he heaved. The coupling stood fast! He cursed and applied more pressure. Exerting all his strength, he tried to push the metal upwards, while the slugs snapped at and gouged the snow at his feet. He knew it would be only a matter of seconds before he was hit. Still the damned coupling would not move.

Suddenly a massive shoulder elbowed him aside. 'Excuse me, sir,' Ox-Jo bellowed, 'but you've really got your arse in a crack. Let Mrs Meier's big son have a go!'

Ox-Jo grabbed the coupling, his big chin thrust out stubbornly, and heaved. Above him Jap fired swift, accurate bursts to both sides, ignoring the slugs howling off the steps, trying to keep the advancing partisans at bay.

Slowly, the coupling began to move. Stuermer grabbed hold, too, exerting the last of his strength. The partisans were almost on top of them: he could hear their wild, excited cries of triumph. If the damned thing did not move soon . . .

They were nearly caught off guard by its release.

'The whoreson's moving!' Jap cried in delight, ducking instinctively as a burst of machine-pistol fire stitched jagged holes in the wood above his wizened face. '*Moving!*'

The lone coach was indeed moving, slowly yet gathering speed with every metre as it started to roll back down the long slope.

'Come on, Ox, what are you waiting for?' Stuermer gasped. He grabbed for a loose coupling which was trailing behind the coach, dragging a stream of blue sparks with it as it struck the metal rails.

Ox-Jo woke up to the fact that they were being left behind. 'Not without Mrs Meier's boy!' he yelled, grabbing hold. A moment later, the cheering Edelweiss troopers dragged Stuermer and Ox-Jo back into the coach as it roared down the steep incline, the sound of firing diminishing by the second.

THREE

'Comrade Marshal,' Captain Popvic said, clicking his heels together and bowing stiffly from the waist, as if he were still an officer of the Royal Guard and not a captain in the eleventh Kozara Brigade.

'Comrade Captain,' Tito said equally formally, half-amused, yet half-puzzled by the tall Serbian who disdained the beard and the deliberately ragged appearance of the typical partisan and instead was as immaculately uniformed as any regular officer.

'We did it!' He held up his thumb in the manner of the English SOE instructors who had trained the brigade in its murderous handiwork. '*Train twenty!*'

'Congratulations, comrade,' Tito said, raising his voice above the racket made by the German planes who were bombing Drvar once again. 'Tell me about it. A cigarette – an English one. You see, our comrades in Moscow are a little backward in their production of cigarettes.'

'Yes, I've always thought that black tobacco of theirs must be produced in the Kremlin's latrines. But if you will forgive me, Comrade Marshal, I shall smoke one of my own.'

He took out his gold-plated cigarette-case and extracted his own special brand. He lit it with due ceremony, while Tito admired his style, and then gave his account of the train wreck.

'How many Fritz dead?' Tito asked after he was finished.

'Nearly one hundred and fifty, I counted them myself.'

'Prisoners?'

Popvic gave Tito his wolfish smile but said nothing.

Tito nodded. 'I understand. Weapons?'

'Two mortars, eleven mg 42s, eighty rifles and twenty pistols, which my brave partisans refuse to give up to the common pool.' He flashed Tito a brilliant white smile.

'Excellent . . . excellent. You have done well.'

'But there is one thing, Comrade Marshal.'

'What is it?' Tito asked, seeing the puzzled frown on the handsome young officer's lean, rapacious face.

'One of the Fritz coaches managed to get away. It was at the far end of the train, and the Fritzes managed to push it down the slope before we could get to them. However, some of their equipment got left behind, like this item.' He held out the climbing iron which he had brought stuck in the back of his gleaming leather belt.

Tito looked at it, puzzled. 'What is so strange about that, Captain? It obviously belonged to some mountain trooper. There are plenty of them in the Balkans.'

'Agreed, Comrade Marshal. But look at the stamp on it.' He handed it to Tito.

The Marshal read the word embossed on it aloud. '*Moskva*.'

'Yes, *Moskva*. In other words, it is a piece of Russian equipment like the two Tommy-guns that they left behind, too. What would German mountain troops be doing with Russian equipment? If you will forgive me, I am afraid our communist comrades in Russia have not yet achieved the quality of production of the Fritzes.'

Tito ignored the dig. 'It is indeed strange. What do they want with Soviet equipment when their own is superior?' Tito waited until the ear-splitting siren of yet another diving Stuka had died away, then he said slowly and thoughtfully, 'Captain Popvic, I am glad that you have brought this matter to my attention. You know, in the years when I was "illegal" before your people picked me up and tortured me—'

Popvic grinned cheerfully. He was not intimidated by the 'your people.' He knew he wasn't going to survive the war anyway. He would die in battle before the great cleansing of the communist army began.

'—I could always sense when there was thick air, as we illegals called it. Some sixth sense has always told me when trouble was brewing. I have the same feeling now and I've had it for days, ever since these damned Fritz attacks commenced.

Drop everything else, Popvic.' He leaned forward urgently and placed his hand on Popvic's arm with unexpected familiarity. 'Find those Fritz mountaineers – *and exterminate them!*'

FOUR

They had been marching down the length of the Dalmatian coast for a week now, sticking to the low coastal mountains, which were already free of snow and only sparsely populated. In theory, the area was still under the combined German-Italian control, but Colonel Stuermer was taking no chances; he had a feeling that although they and their Italian allies might control the area by day, it belonged to the partisans after darkness had fallen.

For that reason he avoided the few mountain villages and hamlets they encountered, only allowing his hungry troopers to forage for food – a few chickens, a handful or two of stolen eggs, twice a black piglet – at night. The farmers and the peasants, he reasoned, would put the thefts down to the partisans.

Stormtroop Edelweiss had traversed the whole length of the coastal mountains from Rijeka and were now coming down into the foothills above the port of Split, which was still firmly in German hands. Not once had they encountered partisans, but Stuermer knew they were not far off. Twice they had spotted the faint pink glow of their camp fires higher up in the mountains to the east, and once they had been startled out of an exhausted sleep by the slow chatter of a machine-gun, which Stuermer's trained ear recognized as a Bren, one kind of gun supplied to the partisans by the Tommies.

Soon, he knew, they would have to change direction and penetrate the thin partisan outer-screen which must surely cover Tito's mountain kingdom. The thought worried him. It was a big decision to make – to take his 100-odd men deep into the partisan stronghold. On previous deep penetration missions, they had been fighting civilized armies, who had observed, more or less the Geneva Convention and the Hague Rules for Land Warfare. It would be different with the partisan army, who had a century-old tradition of irregular combat dating back to the days of the Turkish occupation: a brutal, bloody tradition in which no quarter was given or expected. There would be no POW camp for the men of Stormtroop Edelweiss if they were captured; Stuermer knew that. The only fate they could expect would be mutilation – and then death.

On the night of the eighth day of their long march, they pitched camp twenty kilometres from Split. Below, the sea sparkled in the setting sun. To the east, as far as the eye could see, the purple-tinged mountains spread out to the horizon. Nowhere was there any sign of human habitation.

Stuermer, standing away from the camp, lowered his binoculars, feeling somewhat happier and more confident. Perhaps it was the solitude of the mountains which was affecting him. For a few minutes longer he watched the purple of the heights turn a darker hue and slowly begin to merge imperceptibly into the horizon. Soon it would be dark.

Stuermer turned and began to walk back to the camp. Ox-Jo was roasting the little pig he had stolen from some unsuspecting peasant an hour before. Caked in mud, its plump little body was already baking deep in the ashes of a fire which he had just extinguished – the flames must not be allowed to reveal their positions.

'Smells good, Ox,' he complimented the sweating, red-faced NCO.

'It'll taste good, too, sir,' Ox said happily. 'Just like a real old pig-killing feast back on the farm. Given some spices – and time – I could have made a nice bit of blood sausage from its blood.'

Stuermer's smile vanished. Time was what they didn't have. He surveyed the scene in camp. Some of his men were sprawled in the short cropped grass with their big mountain boots high in the air, resting their weary feet. Others were busy making little tents for the nights out of their shelter halves, filling them with bracken and fronds, gouging out holes with their knives in which they would rest their hips. It could well have been a peacetime camp on some climbing expedition, but it wasn't. The Tommy guns hanging from the trees everywhere told him that. In spite of the calm of these remote mountains, they were in the midst of total war and these men were soldiers who would kill and be killed when the time came. Stuermer knew he must tell them now what their mission was.

'Greul – Major Greul,' he called.

Greul, a fanatic for personal cleanliness, looked up from the icy mountain stream in which he was bathing naked. 'Sir.'

'Call the men together in five minutes,' Stuermer commanded. 'I want to talk to them before it gets too dark.'

'Sir!' Greul barked, as if he were on the parade-ground back in the *Reich*.

Stuermer sighed. Must the man always be so damned Prussian!

Five minutes later the men were assembled, squatting in the grass, which already was beginning to grow damp with dew, at Colonel Stuermer's feet. Swiftly, the CO outlined the great plan for the attack on Tito's HQ, filling in the top-secret details of the airborne operation before coming to their own role.

'Comrades,' he said hesitantly, 'you know that I do not risk the lives of my men unnecessarily or carelessly.'

There was a rumble of agreement among the men, though Greul's face twisted in a sneer at such softness. There was no higher honour for a soldier than to die for Folk, Fatherland and Führer.

'But sometimes, if the stakes are high, risks must be taken, even if good men die in the process. This time I think the stakes are high enough. If we succeed in our part of the mission, it could well mean that we will win the war in the Balkans.'

Ox-Jo nudged Jap and whispered out of the side of his mouth, 'Here it comes, the *thick* end!'

'What is our role then? The airborne op is only an expensive feint. Long before the paras and the gliders arrive, we will be in position around the caves inhabited by Tito. In the expected confusion and panic, with all available enemy troops rushing to the aid of the garrison in Drvar –' he licked suddenly dry lips and gazed around at their honest, bronzed, expectant faces somewhat hesitantly – 'we will enter those caves and take out Tito. In short, comrades, our job is to kidnap Marshal Tito!'

Some of the men groaned; others gave a surprised whistle. Perhaps Ox-Jo summed up the men's reaction best of all when he growled, *'Is that all! Well, I'll go and piss up my leg ...'*

As he had been promised by Rendulic, their guides into Tito's mountain fastness arrived from Split in the middle of the night. The two men were so skilled in the ways of the mountains that they almost caught unawares the veteran Jap, who was guarding the entrance to the sleeping camp. Just in time their whispered 'Stormtroop Edelweiss, please' in a strangely accented German saved them from a sudden death.

Swiftly, Jap searched them and found them clean save for two villainous-looking knives and a paper packet of pepper (used for blinding their oppenents) each. Without another word, he marched them, hands in the air, to where the CO slept beneath his dew-glistening shelter half.

Stuermer was awake immediately. In the silver light of the half-moon, he stared at the two men wearing the red fez of the Bosnian Muslim minority. From his briefing he knew they were Mujos, members of the 13th SS Mountain Division *Handschar,* the only SS formation with its own Muslim Iman priest and the only one allowed by Himmler to pray to Allah five times a day. But these two men had been employed as guides and undercover agents in the Split area the past twelve months and they were the men who would take Stormtroop Edelweiss in.

He shook hands with the taller Mujo, whose face was dominated by a great curved nose above a straggly moustache, and then with the other one, much smaller and fatter, with a terrible squint in his right eye. (Already Jap had given them their nicknames – Conk and Cockeye.)

Stuermer asked urgently, 'The barges are in position?'

'Yes, Colonel,' Conk answered in badly accented German. 'They are already anchored in the mouth of the River Cetina. They sail, according to our information, tomorrow night, just after midnight.'

Stuermer nodded his approval. 'Good. And the Italian crews?'

Cockeye spat in the grass contemptuously. 'Spaghetti-eaters!' he growled. 'A bunch of old women, afraid of their own shadows.'

'Let us hope so,' Stuermer said, pleased with the information. 'All right, the two of you, find yourselves somewhere to sleep for the rest of the night.'

'Good, Colonel,' they said and slipped away as silently as they had come, leaving Stuermer lying on his back, hands under his head, staring at the pitiless silver of the night sky.

There was no way back. Tomorrow night they were going in.

FIVE

Frogs croaked hoarsely, as they crawled cautiously through the dry reeds which lined the banks of the broad estuary. Above them the moon peeped from behind a black cloud and tinged the water ahead a faint silver. There was sufficient light for them to make out the squat hulks of the two blacked-out Italian motor-barges anchored there.

'Some allies,' Ox-Jo had remarked scornfully when Colonel Stuermer had explained how the Italian garrison of Split and the other coastal ports had been running guns to the partisans for gold ever since their countrymen in Italy had revolted against Mussolini and they had been forced by the German High Command in Jugoslavia to continue the fight. 'With friends like that bunch of macaronis, we don't need enemies.'

'Yes,' Stuermer had agreed ruefully, 'but for this once, they will serve the German cause. Those barges will get us through the partisan outer-screen.'

'Great buckets of shit!' Ox-Jo had cursed, 'I thought we were mountaineers, not pirates!'

Now with Greul's group, guided by Conk, approaching the other barge from the far bank, Cockeye lead Stuermer's men towards the nearside barge. No sound came from the boat, but Stuermer guessed the Italians, though usually careless, would have some sort of look-out, if only to keep an eye open for any German patrol from Split that might find its way to the estuary.

The minutes crawled by leadenly as they came ever closer to the unsuspecting Italians. According to their guide, the tidal race would be over within two hours; then the Italian Navy would start their way up the river to reach their destination and be back on the coast under the cover of darkness.

Stuermer paused and turned to the others crouched in the

reeds behind him. 'Remember, no firing, if possible,' he hissed. 'Knife and club – and remember, too, we need the Italian crew to run the boats for us. You fellers are all right in the mountains, but you've no idea how to handle boats.'

'Never fear, sir,' Ox-Jo whispered behind him. 'We'll sort the wops out, nice and gentle.' He doubled his hamlike fist. 'They've never seen a sleeping pill like this before.'

Stuermer grinned.

Their guide, Cockeye, was not amused. 'Watch,' he warned. 'Ground no good. Plenty of—' he could not find the German word and instead made a sucking noise with his mouth.

'You mean *swamps*?' Stuermer prompted.

'Yes, he right – *swamps*,' their guide said eagerly.

'Don't worry, we'll watch out,' Stuermer said. 'All right, you stay here. The rest of you, follow me.'

They began to squirm their way forward towards the boats.

Gasping from the effort, Stuermer led them forward, thankful for the hoarse croaking of the bullfrogs to cover any noise they made. He could see the barge quite clearly, and above the faint red glimmer of the starboard lantern, he could make out the bent outline of the look-out. Obviously, from his motionless position leaning against the long-old-fashioned Italian rifle, and the way his head was bent, the man was dozing. All to the good, Stuermer thought. Once he had climbed up the anchor chain and got his hands round the man's neck, everything else would be plain sailing; he reasoned that the rest of the crew would be below deck, catching an hour's sleep before they sailed.

'Give me five minutes, Ox,' he whispered to the Bavarian giant behind him, 'then come. I'm going in.'

'*Hals und Beinbruch, Herr Oberst,*' Ox-Jo whispered back.

'Thanks,' Stuermer said. Parting the reeds ahead of him, he started to cover the last twenty-odd metres to the silent, unsuspecting barge. The mission was as good as finished.

Suddenly, the ground gave way beneath him. He gasped with shock as he slipped into the cold, cold mud – up to *his knees! ... his crotch! ... his waist!* Abruptly, he was fighting for his life, the boat forgotten now, as the mud began to suck him under.

'*Sir!*' Ox-Jo whispered urgently behind him.

Stuermer caught himself just in time. In another instant he would have screamed out in absolute panic.

'All right . . . all right!' he gasped, trying to control his terror. 'Work round to the right.'

'But—'

'No buts,' he breathed. 'I'll get out under my own steam ... Nobody else ... this way ... clear?'

'Clear, sir.'

Stuermer forgot the others now. He had warned them, and now he must look after himself – before it was too late. The mud was already beginning to drag him under. He fought the wild desire to thrash around with his arms, and sought something solid to grab in the morass. Nothing, he told himself, Nothing at all. He took a deep, deep breath, concentrating all his strength on his legs and thighs.

An alarming fact flashed frighteningly through his mind: one cubic metre of ordinary dirt weighed at least one ton. Mud must weigh at least double! He was up to his waist in at least three metres of mud!

'*No . . . no . . . no!*' he commanded himself urgently. Gingerly, he started to bend his body forward, his nostrils suddenly full of the stench of the swamp. With his arms outstretched rigidly, from above he must have looked like some latter-day Christ on the Cross. Then he let himself fall forward onto the mud.

He lay there on its stinking, slimy, moving surface, hardly daring to breathe, knowing that if he made one wrong move or too hasty a gesture, he would go under; there would be no way that he could save himself. He whispered an urgent prayer and, trying to keep his upper body perfectly rigid and still, began slowly to raise his legs. His heart beating like a trip-hammer, Stuermer felt as if he were separated from death by a mere millimetre; lying on top of it, its slave, kept from it only by something as tenuous as the will to survive.

Hearing an obscene sucking noise, Stuermer was overcome by a tremendous feeling of elation. *His right leg was beginning to move!* He controlled himself just in time. Any hasty movement and his whole body would keel over, forced deeper into the slime by the change in pressure. Willing himself to do so, his mouth full of mud and his nostrils heavy with its stench, he raised his right leg with infinite patience and slowness, it came free.

Stuermer lay there for what seemed an eternity with his body resting on the quivering surface of the morass, while his left leg remained tightly buried. Again he said a quick prayer and began the terrible, seemingly endless procedure once again.

Once more he lay there gasping in relief, fighting desperately to control his wild breathing. Then he started to crawl forward, arms and legs spread out as far as they would go, making the largest possible body surface.

His slow progress across the surface of the morass seemed never-ending. His body was racked with horrible fears, as the mud swayed and groaned beneath him. Would it never release him? Would he never be able to escape it? And then, as abruptly as he had fallen, he was in icy, deep water and swimming automatically, free from its grip. He had done it! *He had escaped!*

Gasping for breath, his whole body stinking of mud and fear, his limbs trembling with the effort, Stuermer grasped the achor chain of the barge and hung on to it with the last of his strength.

With unexpected quietness for a big man, Ox-Jo appeared out of the night and took hold, too. 'All right, sir?' he asked anxiously.

'All right.'

'No!' Ox-Jo placed a big paw on Stuermer to restrain him. 'You stay here. Hey, yellow turd,' he hissed at Jap, who had just swum around the stern, 'take care of the CO I'm off up.'

Without waiting for his CO's reaction, Ox-Jo grasped the chain with one hand and heaved, a wet sock filled with sand held at the ready in the other. He tugged himself up rung by rung and then pulled himself noiselessly over the wooden balustrade. The sentry slept on.

Ox-Jo grinned evilly in the darkness. 'Little spaghetti-eater take sleepy-time?' he whispered maliciously, creeping forward. The only sound to be heard was the *drip-drip* of water onto the deck. 'Pleasant dreams,' he hissed, raising his black-jack. Next instant he brought it down on the back of the unsuspecting Italian's head. When he lurched forward, Ox-Jo caught him and gently lowered him to the deck, preparing to move on. As an afterthought, he positioned the unconscious man on his side, with his hands beneath his head, as if he were in a deep sleep. 'Dream well, sweet prince,' Ox-Jo whispered, blowing him a juicy kiss as more and more of the Edelweiss troopers started to swarm over the sides noiselessly.

Just as he was going to ring the alarm bell, the watchman on the bridge fell with Jap's knife deeply imbedded between his ribs. The skipper, a sleek-haired young lieutenant, went down as if pole-axed when Ox-Jo's blackjack caught him at the side of his carefully marcelled head.

And then the troopers were everywhere. The half-dressed Italian sailors cowered wild-eyed in their rumpled bunks, staring at the half-naked mud-stained giants who had appeared from nowhere in the middle of the night, Within minutes the barge was taken. The voyage into Tito's mountaintain fortress could commence.

They were on their way . . .

BOOK THREE: CLASH!

ONE

The two motor-barges chugged lazily up the broad river, coloured a dark brown by the water coming down from the mountains, where at last the snow was beginning to melt. At a steady fifteen kilometres per hour, they were steered ever eastwards by the two frightened Italian helmsmen, guarded by Edelweiss troopers. On the decks, the soldiers sat, stripped bare to the waist to let their lean muscular bodies soak in the early May sunshine, and curiously regarded the land on both sides of the Cetina.

The land was fertile, with green fields everywhere flanked by high hedges of sunflowers, obviously meant to keep the plump black pigs from rooting out the potatoes and other crops buried in the rich, black soil. There were plenty of signs of human habitation, too: little straw-roofed white cottages surrounded by tumbledown picket fences, with lazy curls of blue smoke ascending from their chimneys into the bright blue sky.

It was a pleasant, peaceful rural scene, but Colonel Stuermer knew as he surveyed both banks in turn it was deceptive. They were already in partisan country. Three hours earlier they had swept silently, motors turned off, past the place where the Italians normally met the partisans who brought the weapons from them, and had floated for a good half an hour with the current before they had dared to turn on the motors again. Now they were deep in an area where no German patrol had dared to venture for over a year. Somewhere soon, Stuermer knew, they would bump into the partisans' main checkpoint. As he had explained over breakfast to Greul, who was in charge of the other barge, 'Naturally they'll have some kind of a check on the river.'

'Perhaps a patrol boat?' Greul had ventured.

'Perhaps. According to the map the river gets narrower farther on. Maybe they'll have some sort of post there at the narrows. At all events, Greul, we must fool them long enough that we are Russians coming to help the partisans so that we can knock the station out of action.'

'Agreed,' Greul had snapped decisively, finishing his weak Italian coffee with a flourish. 'There must be no survivors, Colonel, to warn that rabble's high command. No survivors whatsoever!'

'*No survivors,*' Colonel Stuermer mused to himself now as he swept the left bank with his glasses once again. Easily said, but what did it mean in practice? Slaughtering young men, cutting them down in the prime of their life. He shrugged and dismissed the thought, for he knew that Greul was right. Instead he concentrated on the task ahead. When would they hit the partisan line?

'This is what I call a gentlemen's war,' Ox-Jo said happily, taking another swig out of his chianti bottle, which he had got from the scared Italians below an hour before. 'My own private yacht, complete with crew, a good bottle of wine, excellent weather. All that's lacking is a nice juicy tart.'

Greedily, Jap watched Ox-Jo's Adam's-apple rise and fall like a lift as he poured down the red wine. 'Hey, watch out with that sauce!' he protested at last. 'You're knocking it back as if it's going out of fashion!'

Ox-Jo took the bottle from his mouth, wiped his blood-red lips and belched pleasurably. 'Yer know, I promised yer mother on her death-bed I would protect her little boy from the evils of drink,' he growled.

'Ballocks,' Jap said, grabbing at the bottle.

Ox-Jo allowed him to take it and shook his head in mock wonder. 'Some people have no shitting manners,' he said mildly as Jap downed a tremendous slug.

'Well, what do you think, Ox?' Jap said finally, giving him back the bottle.

'About what, my little turd?'

'About this lark.' Jap's waving hand indicated both the boat and the far bank.

Ox-Jo shrugged easily. 'We common soldiers aren't paid to think, you asparagus Tarzan. That's left to the officers and gents.' He nodded at Colonel Stuermer on the bridge. 'Oh, you know the CO. He's not one of those glory hunters like Greul, always after some new kind of tin collar,* even if a lot of good lads have to hop so that he can get it. If anyone can get us in and out, you can bet yer life it'll be the CO. Stuermer'll do it.'

'Yer, you're right there,' Jap agreed. 'The Old Man'll see us through.' He lay back and, closing his eyes, began to soak up the sun.

The jolt as the leading barge struck the obstacle jerked Colonel Stuermer out of his sun-induced midday doze. He opened his eyes with a start. The barge had just turned a tree-lined bend in the river and run straight into a rusty but stout iron chain stretched across the brown water. They had bumped right into the partisan checkpoint!

Stuermer was awake at once. Springing to his feet, unslinging his Russian Tommy-gun as he did so, he clattered down the steps from the bridge. On the deck, his troopers were grabbing for their shirts and weapons in a sudden frenzy of action. Stuermer pushed through them to the bow.

It was the partisans all right. Already a little rowing boat was pulling out from the collection of rough huts which lined the left bank, filled with armed men in fur caps. *Partisans*! Stuermer forced himself to smile, lowering his Tommy gun until it was hidden from sight. Out of the corner of his mouth, he whispered to Ox-Jo and Jap, who followed him to the bow, 'Not one of them is to get away.'

'Right, sir,' Ox-Jo whispered back. He snapped off his

* A decoration.

safety catch with a soft click. 'The hairy-assed buggers'll be gargling with their own piss in a minute.'

The rowing boat came nearer. Meanwhile, more fur-hatted men, hung with belts of ammunition, grenades attached to their equipment everywhere, had come out of the huts and were staring curiously at the stalled barges. Stuermer said a quick prayer. So far they were just curious, not aggressive. He hoped that Greul was being smart enough at this moment to start sending his men over the side concealed from the watchers, to tackle them in surprise.

Suddenly the rowing boat came to a stop. One of the partisans, his fur cap set at a rakish angle, a German Schmeisser hanging across his chest, rose to his feet and, cupping his hands around his mouth, called in broken Italian, '*Dove italiano teniente?*'

Stuermer breathed a sigh of relief. Obviously they knew about weapons shipments. What they did not know was that the Italian lieutenant was long dead. He cupped his hands to his mouth and called back, '*Nyet, nyet,*' in his best Russian, '*Ya russkì!*'

'*Ay-ouch-nem ... ay-ouch-nem,*' Ox-Jo supported him with a few words of the *Volga Boatman's Song* in his atrocious Russian, *ay-ouch-nem ...*'

'*Russki?*' the partisan spokesman echoed increduously.

'*Da, da, tovarischì! Russki.*' Stuermer forced himself to smile broadly even though his nerves were tense. Had Greul got his men over the side now? A couple of more minutes and the game would be up.

The partisan turned round awkwardly and bellowed the information in Serbian to the men standing on the shore. It was greeted by a loud cheer and the waving of rifles and fur caps in the air. To his horror Stuermer saw one of them break away and run to one of the huts from whose roof glistened silver, a radio aerial. Stuermer knew he could wait no longer. The man might well be on his way to radio the news that the Russians had arrived to headquarters.

He ripped up his machine-pistol and fired from the hip.

The man paused almost leisurely at the door to the hut, as if he had remembered something and wanted for a moment to think it out. He tried to hold the wood for support. Suddenly his legs sagged beneath him, as if the sinews had been slashed. He went down on his knees and then flopped forward onto his face.

For one long moment nothing happened. They – the Italians at the wheel, the partisans – were frozen in position like actors at the end of the third act of a melodrama. Then the partisan standing in the boat screamed something. The rowers strained at their oars. On the bank the partisans scattered wildly, firing as they ran. Ox-Jo pressed the trigger of his machine-pistol. The standing man screamed, clutched his ripped-open stomach and pitched over the side into the water. Ox-Jo fired another burst. Wood chips flew high into the air. A sudden line of holes was stitched in the boat's side. In an instant it was sinking, filled with dead and dying men, their blood colouring the water pink.

Stuermer did not wait to see it sink. He swung round again and fired a quick burst at another partisan running for the radio shack. The man slammed into the nearest tree, as if kicked by a mule, and slithered down its length, dragging bloody trails along its bark.

'Grenade, Jap ... for Chrissake, a grenade at that radio hut!'

The little half-breed dropped his Tommy gun and pulled a stick grenade from his boot. Grunting, he pulled out the pin but waited a moment while the fuse fizzed before hurling it with all his strength at the hut. It vanished in a ball of fire.

'Over the side! Everybody over the side!' Stuermer cried above the snap and crackle of the furious small arms fire. 'Nobody's to get away!'

Slugs were now thwacking against the barges' wooden sides. Spurts of water shot up everywhere. Stuermer ignored the bullets. Holding his Tommy gun high, he dropped over the side and struck out one-handed for the bank, followed by the rest of his men. He raced with giant strides for the huts, dripping water as he ran. A cross-eyed partisan tried to stop him. Stuermer jammed the butt of the machine-pistol into his face. He went down with a howl. Stuermer sprang over his writhing body. To his right a partisan snapped off a burst. Stuermer dodged just in time. Behind him there was a cry of pain. One of his men had been hit. Stuermer ripped off a burst from the waist. The partisan was flung right round by the impact of a shot at close range. He went down as if pole-axed.

The entire line of Edelweiss troopers tackled the huts, leaping over the crumpled bodies of their own comrades and the dead partisans, firing and shouting obscenities as they charged. Stuermer rushed for the door of the nearest hut. A mournful face beneath a shaven head appeared. The partisan had a pistol in his hand. Stuermer pressed the trigger of his own machine-pistol. *Nothing happened!* He froze. It had jammed. The partisan grinned wolfishly and took aim deliberately. Stuermer fumbled frantically with the trigger. He could see the partisan's face tighten as he prepared to shoot.

Behind him Jap yelled, 'Out of the way!' Pushing the CO to one side, he fired a tremendous burst from the hip. The partisan died before his face could express any other emotion. As he fell dark astonishment remained in his eyes.

Jap sprang over him and smashed into the darkness of the hut. Crouched at the door, legs apart, Tommy gun at his hip, he swung from left to right, firing as he did. The frightened, open-mouthed faces of the trapped partisans were transformed into shapeless lumps of gore as they toppled in all directions. A huge shape hurled itself out of the scarlet gloom. The heavy body knocked the little half-breed to the floor among the writhing, mutilated bodies, hands grasping for his skinny throat. Jap gasped and dropped the Tommy gun as red and silver stars started to explode in front of his eyes. He was being strangled to death. Desperately he tried to free himself from that iron grip but failed. He was blacking out.

Abruptly, from far away – so far away that he could

hardly believe that it was happening – he heard a faint pistol shot. For one long moment nothing seemed to take place. Then the body on top of him went limp and that tremendous pressure on his windpipe relaxed. A boot thudded into his skinny ribs and a well-known voice said scornfully, 'Well, come on, you little oriental asshole, don't lie there all day! Get the wind at yer tail!' Grunting, Ox-Jo lifted the dead partisan off him as if he weighed nothing at all. 'Move it!' he bellowed, dragging Jap to his feet.

Sergeant Strugar stumbled out of the rear hut, blood streaming from the wound in his forehead. His whole body shook. The screams of the dying and the wounded were horrible. He knew he must get away. With all his remaining energy he forced himself to run for the safety of the forest. He could hear a shout behind him and bullets hissing through the air sliced through the leaves. He staggered on, gasping with effort and horror, flailing through the branches of the trees, stumbling and almost falling in his panic more than once. Suddenly he stopped, his bloody face contorted with terror. A German was standing up ahead with his back to him but the trooper might turn at any moment and spot him. From behind him the cries of his pursuers were getting ever closer.

He knew there was no other way: he had to tackle the Fritz, even weaponless. Cautiously and noiselessly, he crept up behind the unsuspecting trooper, who was resting after the exertions of the battle. His hands found the trooper's throat. Pressing his knee into the small of the German's back, he squeezed hard. But even as the German fell, he managed to half-turn his body and with his one free hand pressed his index finger into the partisan's eye.

Strugar screamed and relaxed his grip momentarily, letting the German fall to the ground. Then Strugar rallied and aimed a vicious kick at the trooper's head, his own head afire with pain. The German's screams alerted the others. Half-blinded with tears but with speed lent to his feet by fear, Sergeant Strugar blundered deeper into the clutches of the forest until it swallowed him up altogether.

'Damn, damn, damn!' Red-faced and sweaty, Stuermer cursed and slammed his fist against the tree trunk as the sounds of the fugitive died away altogether. He flashed a murderous look at Greul, who was panting hard from the fight and the subsequent chase. 'Why didn't you get on the stick quicker—' He caught himself. Now it didn't matter. The man had got away. He would undoubtedly alert his superiors – wherever they might be – that they had been attacked by a mysterious bunch of Russian civilians.

Stuermer turned to Ox-Jo, who had just come lumbering up, already clutching his loot, a bottle of plum brandy, in his free hand. 'Well,' he demanded,' don't just stand there holding that bottle in your hand as if contained damned mother's milk. Report!'

Ox-Jo clicked his heels together, the smile vanishing from his broad face instantly. He could see how worried the CO was. 'Two of our men killed, sir; four wounded.'

'Seriously?' the Colonel enquired quickly, knowing that any man seriously wounded would have to be left behind to the mercies of the partisans.

'No, sir. Flesh wounds the lot. I'd call them scratches, those putty pricks call—'

—'And the partisans?' Stuermer cut him short.

'All dealt with.'

'Liquidated?' Greul butted in.

Ox-Jo nodded.

Stuermer made his decision. 'All right, Sergeant-Major, round up the Stormtroop and let's get back to the boats. The quicker we get out of here the better. If that partisan manages to get through safely, he'll rouse the whole damn countryside against us. At the double now!'

'At the double, sir!' Ox-Jo bellowed dutifully. He ran back to where the troopers were looting the huts, tossing in incendiary grenades once they had taken everything they could find.

Hastily, the men of Stormtroop Edelweiss ran back to the river. Then they came to a sudden stop. The barges were already vanishing around the bend. Two bodies in civilian clothes floating face down in the muddy-brown water gave mute testimony of what the Italians had done; they had killed the guards while the fight had been going on in the huts and the forest.

'What now?' Greul barked.

Stuermer bit his lip, saying nothing. For a moment he stood there in mute shock; then he waved to Cockeye. 'We march,' he said harshly. 'Lead us . . .'

TWO

The Citadel buzzed with activity. Partisan staff officers hurried back and forth, with urgent messages in their hands, their faces pale and tense. Telephones rang incessantly. Radios hummed and their operators sweated beneath the tight earphones. Outside couriers caked in mud and dust, came skidding to a stop on their motorbikes, bearing new tidings of catastrophe from the Front, and map officers placed fresh identifications on the big wall map already covered with a rash of red signs indicating German units.

Tito sat in one corner of the map room, seemingly oblivious to the hectic activity. He smoked his pipe quietly, like some elderly uncle guarding his favourite chair by the fire but playing no part in the life of the family to which he belonged. With cool detachment he observed the flustered staff officers as they raced back and forth or stood in a tense group whispering urgently to one another.

By now he knew that the Germans had attacked the perimeter of his defences near the coast in some strength. Some of the local section commanders on the west flank had definitely panicked. In due course, he would see that they were shot, but that would be afterwards. For the time being he would allow them to continue crying out for reinforcements from the three proletarian corps grouped around Drvar. But that was all. His staff officers, naturally, had pleaded with him to send help, and a worried Chief-of-Staff had looked across at him a couple of times almost pleadingly.

Tito knew he had to make a decision soon. If he did send help, it would weaken his central position. The Fritzes, whose transport was much superior to his, might well then attack his eastern flank and he'd have a devil of a job to whip his army through to the mountains to face the new danger. Perhaps the Germans had different plans altogether? Hadn't they been bombing Drvar all day again, this time using their new gliderborne bombs as well as the dive-bombers?

Almost reluctantly he stubbed out the cigarette he had been smoking in his little pipe and patted his dog. 'Comrades,' he said, his cool voice cutting through the tension in the room, 'may I have your attention, please?'

The hubbub ceased immediately.

'This message will go out to all sector commanders on the Western Flank,' he said decisively. 'Make a slow fighting withdrawal into the mountains. Keep casualties low. No bogging down. Rather run than fight.'

The officers gasped, incredulous. It had taken them nearly a year of hard fighting in the face of severe enemy opposition to establish the Western Flank.

'There will be no change in the positions of the three proletarian corps,' he continued. 'I have decided that this is not the key German offensive. Let the Fritzes have the ground, if they think it is so important. We can always take it back from them if we wish. Bodies – those of our soldiers, comrades – are more important than a few square kilometres of rock.'

He let the information sink in before adding, 'Now, comrades, why are the Fritzes launching this attack? For a bit of mountainside, do you think? No, no, comrades. This is not the big offensive. This is a feint. They are trying to fool us. They are trying to draw away our main strength from here to the Western Flank. But why? That I don't know. But I have a definite suspicion.' He smiled at their worried faces. 'Do not worry. We have survived worse than this in the past three years. We'll beat them, never fear.'

They smiled, somehow relieved. Everyone there knew that time and time again the Germans had announced that the man facing them was defeated and on the run, but somehow he had always managed to fool the Fritzes and fight on. Tito was unbeatable.

'Now, comrades,' the broad-faced leader continued, noting the look of new hope on their worried faces, 'I want all airfields more closely watched – especially those at Kraljevo, Zaluzani and Zagreb. I want an immediate report of any massing of transport planes – those Ju52s and Condors of theirs – whatever function they are supposed to play. I want the liaison missions to find out the situation with the paratroops in Southern France and Italy. I want . . .'

Tito rapped out order after order, keeping his staff officers scribbling frantically on their pads and couriers hastening to the outer door in their droves.

Finally he paused for breath and wiped his lips. 'Now then, what do you hear from Captain Popvic?'

The Chief-of-Staff was caught off guard. 'Captain Popvic? Why, the last I heard from him he had taken his company down to the Cetina.'

'*The Cetina?*'

'Yes, Comrade Marshal. Some story about Russians in the boats that the macaronis use to sell us their weapons. You know that business—'

'Yes, I know, get on with it,' Tito interrupted impatiently.

'Well, the Russians attacked our post and only one man got away. Apparently Popvic thought –' The Chief-of-Staff's voice trailed away. Tito was no longer listening.

Tito frowned, alone with his thoughts, while the rest of them stared down at him and the telephones jingled unanswered. The Chief-of-Staff was a Stalinist; he was not. When the Fritzes had occupied the country in 1941, Stalin had declared, 'Jugoslavia no longer exists.' Although he was a loyal communist, he had been a patriot first. He had defied the Soviet dictator once by forming the National Liberation Army, and he had defied him again by accepting aid from the capitalists – the English and the Americans. It was only much later that Stalin had sent his own military mission to the partisan HQ, and Tito had always had the impression that the Russians were there to spy on him rather than to aid him. Now Russians had apparently turned up within his own territory and had fired on his men. What did it mean? What was Stalin's game, if they had in fact been sent by him?

'Get me the Russian mission,' Tito snapped, suddenly breaking the heavy silence.

A few moments later the aide handed him the phone. 'The Russian mission, Comrade Marshal.'

Tito grabbed the phone and spoke in the fluent Russian he had learnt as a POW in Austria during the First War. The voice at the other end was polite but wary. No, the head of the mission was not there. He had gone to visit the Western Flank.

Tito grunted. Was the subordinate's explanation for the absence of his chief a convenient excuse? 'Do you know anything about the presence of Russians dressed in civilian clothes in the National Liberation Army's area?' he rapped.

There was a moment's hesitation at the other end. Tito wondered if it signified anything more than the fact that the Russian at the other end was merely collecting his thoughts. Then the Russian said, 'I know nothing of any Russians in your area, Comrade Marshal, and I am sure my commander does not know, either.'

Tito rammed down the phone without another word, his pug jaw set stubbornly. What was going on? First Germans apparently armed with Soviet weapons, now mysterious Russians appearing on the Cetina. What did it mean? He did not know the answer, but of one thing he was sure – the thick air was getting ever closer. Something was going to happen soon . . .

THREE

The sniping had begun on the second afternoon after they had left the Cetina. They had been marching through a narrow trail, bordered on the right by the river and on the left by a thick pine wood, when the heavy afternoon silence had been broken by the dry crack of a rifle, like a twig snapping underfoot. A couple of metres behind Stuermer, who was leading the long strung-out column, a trooper yelped with pain and clapped his hand to his suddenly bloody shoulder.

Stormtroop Edelweiss reacted instinctively, throwing themselves into the drainage ditch facing the wood and blasting out with a tremendous volley so that the pines came tumbling down like a heavy green rain. Then they had waited, until Stuermer had raised his cap above the ditch with the aid of a stick as a bait. No takers. The sniper had vanished.

Later that day, when they had set up camp and were beginning to cook their evening meal before it got too dark and they would have to extinguish their fires, another single shot had rung out and one of his troopers had pitched head-first into the fire, a neat hole drilled through the centre of his forehead. A worried Stuermer had doubled up his sentries throughout the night, thinking that the reappearance of the sniper indicated an all-out partisan night attack. But when the dawn had come, it had revealed nothing.

Now, at midday on the second day, after two more casualties due to the mysterious sniper, Stuermer was angry and worried. 'I can't understand it, Greul,' he said to his second-in-command, who marched at his side at the head of the wary column, now strung out in regular battle order, alert and waiting for the sniper to strike again. 'If that man who escaped at the river has already contacted his pals and they have something to do with that damned sniper, why not a full-scale attack? According to Intelligence, their Fifth Proletarian Corps is located no more than thirty kilometres from here. What is to stop them from sending a whole battalion to attack us instead of one single sniper?'

'Perhaps it's some local partisan unit?' Greul suggested, wiping the sweat from his brow. 'And they don't have the strength to attack us. They are harassing us, that's all.'

'If that's so, why attack us in the first place? We could be another partisan outfit in these civvies. How could they know that we are the enemy, eh?'

Greul remained silent, as puzzled as his CO.

'No, Greul, I don't like it one bit. I think the sooner we get away from the delta and up into the high mountains—' Stuermer indicated the glistening peaks of the snow-topped mountains in the far distance – 'the better. This country is too open for me.'

'I agree there, sir, but how long do you estimate it will take us to reach them?'

'Well, if we don't have any more trouble than the odd pot-shot from that bastard, my guess is we'll reach them tomorrow evening.'

The afternoon passed leadenly. The heat was oppressive. The sun was a glaring red ball in the bright blue sky, casting diagonal beams of light through the high bushes which grew on both sides of the trail in lush profusion. Stuermer sensed trouble. The site was a perfect place for an ambush. For hours now they had been marching through an area in which a whole army could have concealed itself easily, yet nothing had happened, except for the crack of that damned sniper's rifle twice.

The whole business was beginning to get on Stuermer's nerves. He had the feeling that they were being watched all the time, and it took an effort of will not to turn every few minutes and check whether or not they were being followed down the narrow trail. In spite of the burning heat, he felt a permanent cold chill run up and down his spine, which made him want to shiver.

As they slogged on, angry, sweating and tired, Stuermer

considered several plans for rooting the sniper out. He could leave a patrol behind to ambush him as he left his hiding place to follow them. But he dismissed that as too risky. They might be attacking a small patrol, and he couldn't afford to lose the men. For a few minutes he toyed with the idea of sending out scouts on both sides of the track, but that, he concluded, would mean they would be hidden from the main body by the thick lush bushes and would be exposed to individual attacks.

For a moment or two he forgot the plans and asked himself once again what the sniper – or snipers – was trying to achieve? He was neither holding up nor slowing down the column. There were four casualties so far, and apart from the dead man, they had all been lightly wounded so that they had been able to keep up with their comrades, Within twenty-four hours Edelweiss would be in the mountains, bare of any vegetation in which a sniper could conceal himself, and that would be that. What would the sniper have achieved? Nothing save a handful of wounded men. Stuermer tugged at the end of his handsome, chiselled nose angrily. This damned gadfly of a mysterious sniper was getting under his skin. It was time he was swatted.

He turned to the trooper marching behind him at the regular five-metres distance, common under battle conditions. 'Soldier, pass it back. Sergeant-Major Meier and his running mate up here. The two guides as well.'

'Yessir.' The trooper turned back to his neighbour. 'Pass it on. Ox-Jo and Jap – and those two guides – up front, at the double.'

'Ox, Jap, Conk and Cockeye ...' The cry went down the column until finally it reached the four men concerned.

'What is it, sir?' Ox-Jo gasped, breaking into a walk as he reached a grim-faced Stuermer. 'Are the officers and gents going to invite us common soldiers to tea – with finger bowls?' He stuck out his little finger – the size of a small sausage – at an exaggerated angle, as if he were holding a cup.

'Knock it off, Ox,' Stuermer rapped. 'I'm in no mood for what you consider humour at this moment.'

Ox-Jo's grin vanished. 'The sniper, sir, I know. It's getting us all down. If we could only see the shitty bastard.'

Stuermer nodded. 'Exactly. Now listen, Ox, I'm not ordering you to go, I'm asking you—'

'To volunteer, sir,' Ox cut him short. 'Well, I'm volunteering, me and this little Asiatic turd at my side. What do you want us to do?'

'See that bend up there? Once we're round it, I want you and your party to go like hell for, say, five hundred metres and then off into the bushes – the ones nearest the river. Set yourself up in a likely spot and wait for him – or them. Give 'em a blast. No messing. Shoot the bastards and don't bother with prisoners.' His jaw hardened angrily. 'Then get the hell out of there and back to the column at the double. We need you.' His voice softened a little. 'And don't take any unnecessary risks, Ox, do you hear?'

'I hear and read you loud and clear, sir,' Ox-Jo said happily. 'Never fear, they're not gonna get Mrs Meier's handsome son that easily.'

Five minutes later they were round the bend and the four troopers were pelting madly for the cover of the bushes. In an instant they vanished into the thick greenery, and all was silent again when the weary column trudged past.

The little ambush was not to work out as Stuermer had planned it. When the four men plunged into the bushes, they saw immediately that they had chosen the wrong spot. Behind the fringe of outer bushes bordering the road, was a well-defined, broad path.

Cockeye, who in spite of his defect had excellent sight, bent and said, 'Look, Germans – tracks.'

Ox-Jo, feeling somewhat naked in the middle of that secret path, bent at his side.

The Bosnian pointed with a dirty finger. 'Wheel tracks –

still fresh.' He touched the soft earth. 'Horse hoofs.'

Ox-Jo nodded. There were imprints of unshod horses, the kind the partistans might use to draw their little covered carts, clearly visible.

Cockeye straightened up. 'Three wagons – going that way,' he pointed ahead.

'Not many,' Jap said. 'Just three of them.'

'Enough to give you a hero's death,' Ox Jo growled, his brow creased in thought.

It was clear now how the unknown sniper had kept up with them. This path must run parallel with the track the column was using. It must have been simplicity itself for the sniper to have doubled along, concealed by the outer bushes, and taken a shot at them. Now it would be equally simple for them to stake out the path and wait for him to come running right into their arms. But the fresh tracks worried him. The carts that had passed this way had obviously been heavily laden. He could see that from the depth of the tracks and the way that, here and there, the wheels had scoured the roots of the bushes a gleaming white as they had bumped against them.

'What you thinking, Ox?' Jap asked, breaking the tense silence.

'This, bird-brain. Perhaps they put that sniper in to delay us because they're preparing something hot for us up ahead.'

Jap nodded. 'That sounds sensible, even from a thick-headed Bavarian barn-shitter like you.'

Ox ignored the remark. 'If that's the case, why worry about the sniper? Isn't it more important to find out what the shits are planning for us up ahead?'

Conk spoke for the first time, wiping the dew from the end of his enormous red beak, which was now swollen and thick with the cold he had caught during the fracus at the river, 'Ambush – my guess,' he said nasally. 'Up ahead – difficult country, perhaps.' He shrugged. 'Don't know. But might be good spot for ambush.'

Ox-Jo made up his mind. He would disobey the CO's

order. 'Come on,' he commanded, slinging his Tommy gun. 'Let's get the lead out of our asses.'

'Where we going, Ox?' Jap demanded as Ox-Jo set off.

'To find out if Santa Claus is waiting up there to give the lads a nice present,' Ox-Jo said scornfully to the little man trotting at his side. 'What did you think, short-ass? *Now move it!*'

FOUR

They began to crawl. The bushes were beginning to thin out but still offered them some cover. The path rose steadily, causing them to sweat heavily with the effort of the climb and the heat. Just before they came to the top, Ox-Jo indicated with a hand sign that they should stop. He crawled on alone, raising his big head carefully over the rise.

Down below, the trail along which Stormtroop Edelweiss would have to march if they were to reach the mountains ran over a wide bubbling stream, which in its turn undoubtedly ran into the Cetina. Crossing it was a rickety wooden bridge. It was not the bridge, however, which barred the mountaineers' further progress and caused Ox-Jo to bite his bottom lip in frustration. It was the collection of wooden huts, made of roughly hewn logs, on the far side of the creek, and the underground bunkers that lay in front of them, guarding the exit to the bridge. It did not take a mind-reader to guess what was going to happen if Stormtroop Edelweiss continued on its present collision course.

Swiftly, Ox-Jo threw a glance to the right and left of the fortified settlement and groaned inwardly. The position had been picked with great care, he could see that. To his left the rock-wall rose at an impossible angle from the trail. It would take a master climber to tackle that face, even under peacetime conditions, not to mention under enemy fire. To his right, the gleam of water in the coarse grass on both sides of the stream told him that it was swampland. He, like all the rest of the assault party on the barges that night in the estuary, had had enough of swamps.

Suddenly his attention was caught by the appearance of an elderly, yellowed man coming from one of the bunkers. He strolled to the far end of the rickety bridge – obviously to begin a spell of sentry duty – as if he had all the time in the world. Then he came to a halt and stared dully at the fast-running water below, his Tommy gun slung diagonally across his back.

Ox-Jo studied him carefully, wondering how many more of his kind were hidden in the huts and in the bunkers beyond. Slowly, it dawned on him that the partisan looked different from the ones they had fought at the river post. He was clean-shaven, and although he wore a dark fur cap like the ones they had slaughtered in the huts, there was no sign of the familiar red star badge. In its place was a gleaming silver badge which appeared at that distance to be topped by a crown. Ox-Jo frowned, puzzled. 'Commiee partisans – with a crown?' he said to himself. 'That's sodding funny.' Making up his mind, he turned and beckoned wordlessly to Cockeye, who had the keener eyes of the two guides. *Come*, he mouthed the words silently.

The little Muslim crawled up beside him and peered carefully over the top of the rise.

'What do you make of that arsehole?' Ox-Jo whispered in his ear. 'Look at his cap.'

The little, brown-faced Bosnian took only a few seconds to make his identification. 'Vojvodan Kosta Recanac,' he announced firmly.

'Eh? And what's that when it's at home?'

'No what,' Cockeye explained. '*Who*.'

Ox-Jo was as puzzled as ever. 'For crying out loud, Cockeye, let's have that in clear-text, will ya! I've had a shitting hard day as it is.'

Cockeye rolled over on his back and stared up at Ox-Jo's big red face with his terrible squint. 'Vojvodan Kosta Recanac, he famous Chetnik.'

'Yer, some people can sodding well break their noses when they fall on their arses,' Ox-Jo snapped irritably, apropos of nothing. 'What you tell me?' he aped the little man's broken German.

'I tell you he fight German. Then he fight Commie – Tito, you understand?'

'Yer, me understand. Get on with it.'

'English help Tito, no Chetniks. Lot of problems for Chetniks. No know what do.'

'So? What else is new?'

'So,' Cockeye answered, Ox-Jo's irony wasted on him, 'some Chetniks fight German. Some fight commies. Some fight English. Some fight everybody—'

'Shall we continue the lesson tomorrow morning? Great pails o' piss, man, belt it out!'

'And Vojvodan Kosta Recanac – he famous Chetnik –' the little guide repeated the information – 'he turn bandit.'

'*Bandit?* Here in the middle of the shitting partisans?' Ox-Jo exploded.

'Yer, best place. No German to bother him. Only shitty-assed civilians, scared of partisans. He find outway place like here ...'

Swiftly, in his fractured German, he explained how the partisan leader set up these fortified villages in the remoter parts of Tito's stronghold and took what he could from the frightened civilians in the fashion of some medieval Rhenish robber-baron; he then moved on to find some other likely site, once Tito's troops, who had other things to do than deal with this minor sore on their perimeter, made an appearance.

When he had finished his explanation, Ox-Jo said, 'But by now, they'll know we're armed. From the snipers. They'll have told them. They won't want to tackle a company of armed men.'

'Why not?' Cockeye slapped the butt of his Tommy gun. 'In mountains today, you get five cows, two acres of land, fine fat woman for gun like this. Gun more important money. Vojvodan Kosta Recanac want guns. Much wealth.'

'But he's gonna to have to make a fight for them, man,' Ox-Jo protested. 'Hell, he's gonna get his arse kicked if he tries to take our weapons away! Besides, we can always make a detour. I know that position down there is pretty good, but we don't need to take it. We could sort those shitty snipers out and back up until we could find anot—'

His heated words were drowned by a heavy explosion to his rear. A thick black mushroom of smoke was ascending rapidly into the leaden sky from the direction of the trail.

'*Shit ... shit ... shit,*' Ox-Jo cursed. He knew instinctively what had happened. The snipers had blown the trail behind Stormtroop Edelweiss. Now there was no way back. The sudden snap and crackle of small arms fire told him the next moment that the snipers were now going into action, driving the troopers towards the bridge – and the trap – like sheep-dogs herding their stupid charges to the slaughter.

FIVE

'*Wheeh!*' The bullet howled off the rock-face as the trapped Edelweiss men flung themselves down in the dust on both sides of the track, burying their heads as low as they could while the slugs zapped frighteningly just above their quaking bodies.

Stuermer cursed. He knew from the explosion of the land mines a couple of hundred metres to their rear that there was no way back. But what lay up front of them? Instinctively, he knew that there was trouble waiting for them ahead. Why else were the snipers intensifying their efforts now, after twenty-four hours of casual sniping? Somebody had got them by the short and curlies in a particularly nasty fashion.

'*Sir!*' a familiar voice called.

He raised his head cautiously. Ox-Jo's broad face peered out of the bushes some twenty metres away. 'What is it? Trouble?'

'Plenty, sir. Gimme covering fire and I'll come over and tell you the bad news.'

Stuermer didn't hesitate. The unexpected always worked in combat, he believed. Springing to his feet, ignoring the slugs whining all around, he sprayed the bushes to their rear from which the snipers' fire was coming, whipping from left to right like a Western gun-fighter in some pre-war film.

Ox-Jo and his group didn't need a second invitation. Taking advantage of the diversion, they sprang out of their hiding place and pelted across the track. Ox-Jo skidded to a halt next to his CO and dropped to his knees. 'Enough of the performance, sir,' he gasped. 'We're here!'

Stuermer dropped in the same moment that a bullet whacked into the rock-wall just above his head. 'All right, you big rogue, give me the bad news.'

Ox-Jo reported their discovery.

'And there's no way to deal with this character?' he asked when Ox-Jo was finished. 'I mean, we've got some gold to grease palms.'

'In a pig's arse, sir! According to our tame Muslims, he's after bigger stuff – our combined arsenal. Apparently it'll bring a lot of marie* on the partisan black market. Hell, these Jug bastards would rather shoot somebody than get rid of their love juices. What a funny lot!'

'You can say that again, Ox,' Stuermer agreed. 'And what does it look like at that bridge?'

Ox-Jo filled in the details.

Stuermer pondered the information for a moment. 'So that means we can't go backward and we can't go forward, eh?'

'Looks like it, sir.'

Stuermer rolled on his back in the dust and stared at the sheer rock-wall to their left.

Ox-Jo followed the direction of his gaze and shook his big head. 'No way, sir!' he snorted, reading the CO's mind. 'All you'll get for that effort is a dirty big slug between the crown jewels.' He grabbed the front of his trousers with an agonized expression on his face to make his meaning clear. 'O, la, la, ain't I got a high voice, all of a sudden! Sir, nobody could tackle that in daylight.'

'Who's talking about daylight?' Stuermer said, his mind racing with new ideas.

'*Darkness!*' Ox-Jo exploded.

'Why not?'

'*Sir!* You know me – I'm very tame. I wouldn't try to rock the boat – and after all you are a senior officer and gentleman – but with your permission, that is a crock of shit! Tackle that – under the cover of darkness. No, sir, that's an open invitation to suicide.'

Stuermer looked at him, his face tense and serious. 'What else is open to us, Ox? We can't go forward, we can't go backwards – we can only go *upwards*.'

* Slang for money.

'Yes,' Ox-Jo commented with wry cynicism, 'and disappear up our own assholes – *fer ever!*'

'All right,' Colonel Stuermer said, 'we're going to do it like this. Major Greul, you've got to keep them occupied somehow.' He ducked as another slug howled off a rock just above his head.

'Sir. But why don't you let me—'

'*No!*' Stuermer cut him short firmly. 'If anyone's going to do this, it's going to be me. I'm the oldest and the most experienced climber. I got you all into this mess, and I'm going to try, at least, to get you out of it.' He turned to an expectant Ox-Jo and Jap. 'Do you want to come with me? I can't ga—'

'Not another word, sir, or me very heart will begin to bleed,' Ox-Jo interrupted. 'What say you, little oriental turd?'

'What can I say, you big Bavarian bastard? One word to the contrary and I'm minus one set of front teeth.'

'Exactly,' Ox-Jo said easily. 'I'm glad to hear that you're volunteering – without pressure.' He looked at his beloved CO. 'There's two of us you've got, sir.'

Stuermer nodded his appreciation. 'You two rogues are enough. Hell, what could I do with any more of your kind – beat the whole goddam partisan army?'

Greul frowned. 'All right, what do you expect me to do? Just play pigeon for them?'

'Exactly.'

Stuermer glanced at the sky. It was already beginning to darken, earlier than usual today because of the impending storm. That made what they had to do easier and yet more difficult. They would be able to climb under the cover of darkness, but if it rained the climb would be even more perilous. He knew, however, there was no other way out. If they could not manage to get behind the bandits on the other side of the creek, they would be finished. Here on the trail they were sitting ducks. The snipers, now that they were bogged down, would be able to pick them off one by one. If they were not on their way by morning when the snipers would have the advantage of full light, he knew that he would have to write off Stormtroop Edelweiss. Nodding at the two NCOs he barked, 'All right, dummies, do you want to live for ever ... let's go!'

The first twenty metres of the ascent on the rock-face were easy. Stuermer had found a fold that hid him and the other two from the snipers and the bandits further up the trail. Together he and the two NCOs scaled the face with comparative ease. Then their luck ran out.

Above their strained faces, the leaden sky was ripped apart. Lightning zig-zagged with violet fierceness across the sky, casting an angry hue across their strained, sweat-lathered faces. There was a great hush, like some primeval monster drawing in its fiery breath. A crash resounded across the hills. After a momentary pause, the atmosphere became charged with tense, nerve-tingling electricity. Then the rains came, hissing down in great hot drops, splashing against their faces, hitting the rock and turning it into a slippery, dangerous surface.

Stuermer cursed. Conditions could not be worse. One false move and they would be falling to their deaths below. All the same, the heavy, almost tropical rain gave them one advantage: it did hide them a little from the bandit positions as they were emerging from the fold.

Stuermer shook his head violently to free his eyes from the raindrops which threatened to blind him and reached upwards. Behind him he heard the laboured breathing of the two NCOs and he knew he must not let them down; he, one of Germany's foremost climbers, must find the easiest route for them.

His fingers sought and found the kind of hold he was looking for – a jug. He smiled in spite of the pelting rain. It was one of the best holds, especially on such a slick surface. He could insert all five fingers to support himself until he had consolidated his foot friction.

'Over there – to the right,' he gasped, taking the strain. For a moment he was suspended in mid-air, his feet without support, his whole body held by the five fingers of his right hand. His shoulder muscles were on fire, and his fingers felt as if they were being ripped out. In spite of the rain beating down on his face, he broke out into a heavy sweat. Then his searching feet found the hold they needed. He braced himself, gasping in relief.

For one grateful moment Stuermer hung there, trying to control his breathing, shaking his head again to get rid of the raindrops, checking the bandit positions for any unusual movement. They had not spotted the three daring climbers clinging to the gleaming rock-face like crazy, drenched flies. He took a deep breath and reached up to the new fold, perhaps a metre above his head. As he squeezed his long lean body into it, he knew that it was going to be tough to ascend the treacherous surface but, as the same time, he knew that the fold was virtually a chimney and would hide them from any chance upwards glance by the bandits.

Carefully, taking as much time as he dared, he pressed his shoulders against the wet rock and then stemmed his boots on a slight outcrop of stone. He grunted and levered himself upwards. He was on his way.

Metre by metre, as the raindrops pelted down, the three men worked their way up the fold, gasping harshly with the effort, their shoulders afire where the rock had rubbed away the skin, their leg muscles screaming out from the strain. Now Stuermer could see the summit. They had nearly done it. With renewed energy and trying to ignore the burning agony, he wriggled his shoulders another few millimetres up the rock. And then it happened. His body slipped on the glossy surface and he began to fall! Just in time he caught his cry of fear; he must not betray his men.

Stuermer gasped with shock, as if someone had slogged a brutal punch deep into his guts. As abruptly as it had started, his fall stopped. For one crazy moment he hung there, panting, his eyes full of tears of gratitude and relief. The strap of the Russian Tommy gun which he had slung across his chest for the climb had caught in a rock outcrop and the tough Russian leather sling was holding his sixty-five kilos effortlessly

'All right, sir?' Ox-Jo's tense voice whispered from below.

'Just,' Stuermer managed to gasp; then, stronger, 'Give me a minute. I'll get myself out of this stupid mess.'

Gingerly, trying not to upset his very delicate balance, he raised his right foot. With infinite slowness he stretched it towards the rock-wall. Above him the leather strap squeaked ominously. Stuermer said an urgent prayer. Beneath him he heard Ox-Jo gasp in alarm and he knew why. One false move and he would plunge down the fold. Even if the fall did not kill him, it would certainly alert the bandits.

Slowly, feeling his pain-racked body break out in a thick sweat, Stuermer stretched out his other foot. Again the leather creaked. *Would it hold?* His foot found the rock-wall. So far so good. He was halfway there now.

While the rain beat down on his supine body, Stuermer continued his strange, silent war against nature. With his gaze directed at his feet to assure himself that he had a firm footing there, he began to feel the surface behind him for a hold for his shoulders, while above him the leather strap squeaked and creaked threateningly. The strain on it must be tremendous, he knew. *He had to find a shoulder hold! SOON!*

Stuermer took a deep breath and chanced it. His shoulders hit rock. The cruel surface bit into his red-raw flesh. As he clenched his teeth to stifle his cry of agony, warm, salty blood flooded his mouth. In the same instant that the leather strap snapped with a crack like that of a pistol being fired, his shoulders dug into the rock and stayed there. He had done it!

Five minutes later the three troopers, soaked to the skin,

ashen-faced and panting, were lying on the top of the cliff-face above the bandit positions, grinning at each other like idiots.

SIX

Stuermer pressed the trigger. The Tommy gun erupted in his hands. The two men on the bridge, huddled in gleaming ponchos, whirled round in crazy animation. One went over headfirst into the white, rain-lashed water, the other fell to his knees, face upturned to the pelting rain, as if pleading to some cruel god to spare him so terrible a fate. Next moment he slapped down on the bridge, dead, in the same instant that Jap and Ox-Jo opened fire.

The surprise attack from the rear achieved its effect. The bandits huddled behind the huts against the storm went down everywhere, caught completely off guard. Those who were hit screamed with pain while the others bolted for cover, trying to get away from that cruel fire. The three men who had appeared from nowhere, their soaked clothes clinging to their skinny frames, had no mercy. They kept their fingers on the triggers.

'Forward!' Greul bellowed, as the firing broke out. 'After me, *Stormtroop Edelweiss!*' he ordered, springing to his feet.

His blond hair plastered to his skull by the rain, he raced forward towards the bridge. The bunker line erupted in violent flame. Edelweiss troopers skidded to a stop and slapped down into the mud. Greul, as brave as he was fanatical, ignored the murderous fire. Firing to left and right from the hip, he rushed across the rickety wooden bridge, springing over the body of the dead man. A bandit loomed up out of the rain-filled ditch on the opposite side and aimed his rifle, but Greul flung the grenade he held in his free hand before the man could shoot. The partisan howled in agony as the grenade found its mark.

Without pausing for breath, Greul ran on seemingly oblivious to the slugs howling through the rain. While the troopers pelted across the bridge, he slammed his shoulder into the backdoor of the first bunker. the men at the firing slits swung round in surprise to face the lean, avenging giant who had appeared from nowhere. His face contorted, his chest heaving, Greul opened fire.

The slugs tore gaping holes in both man and material. Greul acted as if he had a fever. He could not seem to stop firing, although the first bunker was now filled with only dead or dying men. Finally, an enraged Stuermer shook him violently by the collar, crying above the murderous chatter of the machine pistol, *'Greul ... for God's sake, Greul – they're dead. DEAD!'*

Like a drunkard, Greul allowed himself to be led outside. His troopers were finishing off the bunker line with routine professionalism: first a grenade through the rear-door, followed by a burst of machine-gun fire and then their charge, guns blazing. One after another, the bunkers capitulated or were taken by storm until finally it was all over.

The handful of frightened survivors were lined up against the wall of one of the huts, hands in the air, their eyes filled with fear and a sense of hopelessness; the rain streaming down their ashen, bloodied faces with unrelenting fury.

Stuermer stood back a couple of paces and watched them. At that moment, he could feel sympathy for them. They were not unlike him and his men – like soldiers all over the world this May day in the fifth year of the war. Undoubtedly they, too, had gone to war full of ideals, believing they were fighting for their fatherland, freedom and a better future. These ideals had been long forgotten as time passed and treachery, mindless brutality and greed became the order of the day.

Ox-Jo looked at him, as if he could guess what was going through Stuermer's mind at that moment. He opened his mouth to speak, then thought better of it.

Stuermer answered his unspoken query all the same. 'Shoot them,' he said drily. 'Now.' He turned away and strode back to where their own dead lay, piled in a heap like so many logs of wood.

Behind him the bandits, who had once been patriots,

crossed themselves elaborately, in the manner of the Greek Orthodox Church, as a couple of Edelweiss troopers set up a machine-gun in front of them. There was no fear in their eyes now as the gunner ran in the long belt of gleaming ammunition, merely resignation. Just before he pressed the trigger, they clasped hands.

The troopers buried their dead half an hour later. It was still raining heavily and the clouds hung low so that the grave-diggers seemed to be walking through cotton-wool as they completed their task and then walked over to the burning hut to drop their shovels.

Stuermer looked at the dirty, bearded faces of his men and wiped the raindrops off his own tired face with his sleeve. A cold wind had risen, causing the watching troopers to shiver. Stuermer did not seem to notice as he walked over to the pile of fresh brown earth.

'Comrades,' he said softly, no false pathos in his voice, but merely sad weariness. 'A funeral service is something we don't often bother about in Stormtroop Edelweiss, I know. Mostly we don't have time, but those dead young men beneath us deserve a service – and more. If they were buried back home, sorrowing relatives, officials, the local prominence would have paid their last respects.' He shrugged. 'And their names would have been engraved in gold in the chapel of the nearest heroes' cemetery. Here we bury them in some God-forsaken hole in an area whose very name we don't even know.' He paused, and Ox-Jo could see the tears from his tired eyes falling on the worn mountain boots which they had stripped from the dead soldiers, too precious to be left behind in a mass grave.

Stuermer stared at them, blinking his eyes. What times those boots had seen! The heady progress through the *Erzgebirge* into Czechoslovakia. Two years later, in the summer of '40, another triumphal march through the *Alps Maritime.* Finland and victory at Leningrad two years later. But now the victories were more and more costly. They had left their dead behind them spread out over a thousand kilometres, but still they had marched – through Greece, Persia, half a dozen countries! And for what?

Stuermer continued to stare at the boots. Dust and snow had cracked their leather. Countless kilometres had worn down their nails. Mountainous terrains had forced up their soles. Now they had reached their final destination and were laid to rest; useless, wornout, purposeless, like the lives of the men who had survived. He turned, the tears gone now. 'Leave the boots!' he commanded harshly. 'Nobody is to take them. Understood?'

The subdued, weary men mumbled their agreement.

'All right,' Stuermer snapped almost angrily, 'what in three devils' name are you all waiting for? Sergeant-Major, get control of these men, we're moving out.'

'All right,' Ox-Jo barked. 'Get some pepper in yer keesters! Didn't you hear the CO? We're moving out. Are you going to move or have I to pull yer hindlegs straight for you? *MARCH!*'

Slowly the troopers of Stormtroop Edelweiss started to trudge out of the destroyed hamlet, raindrops streaming down their exhausted, skull-like faces like tears. They didn't look back.

BOOK FOUR: DEATH MOUNTAIN

ONE

The Sergeant turned over the dead body with the toe of his muddy boot. 'All dead,' he announced unnecessarily. 'Dead as doornails.'

The partisans stared mutely at the massacred Chetniks.

'They must have been Russian, Comrade Captain,' the Sergeant said. 'If they had have been Fritzes, they surely wouldn't have killed their allies. What do you think, Comrade Captain?'

Popvic did not answer for a moment. It was not the sight of the dead men which caused him to be silent. In these last three years he had seen enough dead men and undoubtedly he would see a lot more before his own turn came to lie there like a broken doll abandoned by an unfeeling, careless child. No, Captain Popvic was thinking.

He stared at the dead men strewn everywhere – in the bullet-pocked huts, one body lying sprawled over the rail of the wooden bridge – trying to make up his mind, while somewhere the water from a gutter dripped irritatingly. Exactly who were the mysterious Russians? Had they anything to do with the Germans who had managed to escape the train ambush? And what were they doing here in the heart of the partisan area, whoever they were?

His eye fell on the mound of fresh brown earth beyond the first hut. Instinctively, he knew it was a mass grave. He studied the spot for a moment. No cross, however crude, nor anything else which might indicate the religion of the strange intruders. Even the Russian atheists put jam-jars containing pictures of the dead on their graves. But whoever had passed this way had not wanted the last resting-place of their dead to be marked.

Captain Popvic made his decision. 'Get those shovels,' he ordered. 'Dig them up.'

'What?' the men demanded.

'You heard, you stupid peasants!' Popvic bellowed. 'Dig the shits up!'

The men hesitated. Most of them were Serbian peasants, who in spite of their lip service to the communist creed were still as suspicious as their grandfathers had been a century before.

Popvic flushed. He swiped an open hand across the Sergeant's shocked face, as if he were still an officer in the Royal Guard with the right of life or death over his wooden soldiers. 'Get them moving, Sergeant. Do you hear? Dig them them up! At once!'

The Sergeant flashed him a look of undying hate, which Popvic ignored. What did peasant hatred worry him? Perhaps the man would attempt to shoot him in the back one day in the heat of battle. Mentally, he shrugged. Die he would; what did it matter what the manner of his death was?

Thoughtfully, Popvic stared down at the waxen faces of the dead men lying at his feet, trickles of brown earth running down on their already rigid bodies, as the diggers scrambled back so that he could see them more clearly. He bent down and, with fingers that trembled only slightly, began to unbutton the jacket on the nearest corpse. There was a swift, awed intake of breath from his men. Popvic ignored it. Dead men were dead man. Nothing more.

Finally he managed to get the jacket open. The label revealed nothing. It was in Cyrillic characters, obviously Russian. But that, he told himself, meant nothing.

He ripped open the metal buttons of the dead man's shirt while his men continued to stare. He ignored their horrified looks. Let the peasants think what they liked. He must discover the identity of these marauders. He stared at the dead man's naked body. It was tough and muscular, that of a well-nourished, hard-working worker – or possibly a well-trained soldier. But again this told him nothing. Dead, all men were alike. Serbian or Russian, Croatian or German – what was the difference?

Suddenly he lifted up the man's right arm. With his free hand, he pushed back the sleeve of the dirty grey shirt, wrinkling his nose at the sudden smell of sweat that assailed his nostrils. He twisted the arm until he could see the paler, softer flesh of the inner upper-arm, then caught his breath. There it was! A letter and two numbers had been tattooed on the delicate white skin! The blood-group marking, which the Fritzes gave to all their elite units so that casualties could be given the correct blood transfusion immediately when their members were wounded in battle. The dead man was a German all right!

Swiftly he checked with the next corpse. The same tattoo. He, too, was a German. They were *all* Germans in that mass grave. Slowly he rose to his feet and, staring at his expectant men, announced, 'Fritzes, not Russians.'

'Fritzes!' they echoed.

Captain Popvic nodded. He turned to the radio-man. 'Get on to HQ,' he commanded. 'Tell them we've got Germans in our backyard.'

'Yes, Comrade Captain,' the signaller said obediently. 'Anything else?'

Popvic hesitated. *Anything else?* How could he know where the Germans had gone and what their purpose was so deep inside partisan territory?

'Yes,' he said decisively after the pause. 'Signal that we are going after them. It's a matter ... a matter of the highest national importance.' He chuckled, 'Yes, send that. That'll set the cat among the pigeons and make a few of those weak sisters at HQ piss their pants.'

The men chuckled. Captain Popvic was rarely given to the usual partisan obscenities.

Popvic smiled with them and then his smile vanished as quickly as it had come. 'Well, don't stand around! Let's get after them.' He stared up at the snow-capped peaks of the far mountains, now disappearing rapidly into the dusk. 'Once they're up there, we've lost them.'

TWO

It was cold, hellishly cold for May. The icy wind raced across the mountains at eighty kilometres per hour, lashing the blade-like snow particles against the weary troopers' faces. As they climbed higher, icicles began to form on their beards, noses, eyelashes. Every intake of breath stabbed painfully at their lungs, and every step forwards required an effort of will. Only the comradeship of Edelweiss and their confidence in their CO's ability kept them going over the terrible terrain.

More than once, Ox-Jo or Stuermer slung the weapon of some weary trooper who staggered like a punchdrunk boxer over his own shoulders, carring it until the man regained his strength. Once even, Ox-Jo had tossed one of the younger men over his shoulder and trudged through the ankle-deep snow for fifteen minutes or so until the exhausted man had croaked, 'All right, Sarge, you can let me down now. I'm better . . . And, thanks for the ride!'

Stuermer, some twenty metres in front of the rest of the troop, which was now strung out a good half a kilometre across the mountain-face, blinked his eyes free of snow and stared through the white mist. He had been right. The dull glaring mass he had spotted through the snow was a glacier. Damn! he cursed to himself. The heavy snowfall had been bad enough; now they would have to contend with crossing a glacier, too.

Once again he blinked his eyes free and tried to ascertain the breadth of the glacier. As far as he could ascertain, it stretched out far to left and right, barring their further progress. Either they must climb it or they would have to make a detour back down the mountainside.

Stuermer stopped and stared at his men's strained, exhausted faces as they staggered blindly forward, their weary legs hardly able to go on. He knew they were in no shape to tackle the glacier this day. They needed rest and food. He held up his hand.

Greul halted next to him. 'What is it, sir?'

'We're stopping here for the night.'

'But there are still three good hours of daylight left,' Greul protested through cracked, parched lips. But his protest lacked his usual note of arrogance. Stuermer could see that his second-in-command had had enough, too.

'Yes, I know. But the men are beat, Greul.' Stuermer raised his voice above the howl of the wind. 'All right, that's it for today. Fix your shelters for the night, then see what you can do about food.'

'Sentries?' Greul asked.

Stuermer looked at the howling white waste all around him. 'Greul, I think we can dispense with them this night. Let everybody get a good night's sleep. We're going to need all our strength to tackle that glacier tomorrow.' He shook his head. 'Who else is likely to be out tonight in this hellstorm?'

For once Colonel Stuermer was wrong. Stormtroop Edelweiss was not alone on that terrible mountain slope.

For three hours, Captain Popvic and his men had been following their trail. Most of his men were Serbian peasants who were used to the mountains, but the strain was even beginning to tell on them. The stragglers fell farther behind, and there were ever increasing complaints from the weary partisans. The Sergeant, who was new to the brigade, appointed himself spokesman for their complaints. Twice he protested that they had had enough and that they should turn back while it was still light. Now as the snowstorm began to ebb and the dully glaring great glacier to their front loomed out of the white fog like some huge silent liner, the purple-faced NCO stopped in front of Popvic, nearly forcing a collision.

'Watch yer damn step, you oaf!' Popvic flared up, his nerves on edge. 'Are you blind, man?'

The Sergeant ignored his rage. 'No, I can see well enough. But *you* can't.'

Popvic knew the moment had come for a confrontation. If he wasn't careful, the impertinent swine would have the men on his side; normally they were loyal, but now that loyalty was strained by exhaustion. 'And what is that supposed to mean, Sergeant?' he asked icily while the men grouped round them and stared uneasily.

'That you must be blind if you can't see there's a damn great glacier up there. There's no way round it!'

'I see it all right – and I'm happy it's there.'

'But why? We can't get up it or round it.'

'Exactly,' Popvic answered, controlling himself. He wished he were back with the Royal Guard for five minutes; there he could have a man like this rat shot for insubordination. 'If we can't get up it or round it, then neither can the Fritzes. If they do what I expect they will, they'll bed down for the night and hope the weather will improve tomorrow.'

'But you can't expect us to attack in this weather,' the Sergeant cut in brutally. 'We're beat. We haven't eaten for twelve hours. You must be crazy!'

'Attack we will – with or without you, Sergeant.' Popvic's right hand dropped onto his revolver holster, his eyes suddenly narrowed. 'I shall not kill you outright, Sergeant. I shall shatter your right knee cap and we'll leave you behind to die out here.' He shrugged without taking his hand off the pistol holster. 'You might even be strong enough to crawl down to the valley . . . It's possible. But remember this, you'll be a cripple for the rest of your days. They tell me you're something of a ladies' man. What woman would want a cripple in bed, eh?'

The Sergeant's face hardened with anger and fear. 'You wouldn't dare to do that!' He spun round on the others. 'Don't listen to him,' he cried passionately. 'He's bluffing. He wouldn't dare to shoot me. Marshal Tito knows me personally. I was in the Party before the war. We were in Belgrade jail together. He'd never —'

The Sergeant stopped short. Popvic had drawn his pistol and clicked back the hammer. Now it was pointing directly at the enraged NCO's right knee.

'Well,' Popvic asked almost tenderly, 'what is it to be – march or crawl?'

The NCO flashed another look at the men all around him. They were avoiding his gaze and he knew they would not back him up – *yet*. His shoulders sank in defeat.

Wordlessly, Popvic put his pistol back into its holster, then waved his hand and set off. The men began to trudge on after him. The red-faced NCO stood fixedly in the softly falling snow, watching them as they passed in weary silence; then he, too, joined the long line, murder in his heart.

Stuermer crouched in his little igloo. He was cold, but not uncomfortable. The snow blocks, sealed together by the simple expedient of urinating on the joints and letting the urine freeze over, kept out the icy wind. Now all was silent in the camp save for Ox-Jo's heavy snores from two igloos away and the howl of the wind.

They had been unable to start a fire. In the end the weary men had swallowed a mess of wet oatmeal and jam and washed it down with a tot of brandy each, in a canteen of melted snow-water. It had not been much of a meal, but it had warmed them a little. Now they slept, forgetting the misery of the day and what lay before them.

Stuermer snuggled deeper into the inviting warmth of his sleeping bag, watching the flickering of the candle stump, which sent the shadows waving in mysterious profusion every time the wind caught it. Oddly enough, he told himself, and despite his exahustion, he felt at peace. They had overcome the enemy and were once again in the high mountains, where the only challenge came from nature. The bloodshed was over – for the time being. Tomorrow they would conquer the glacier; thereafter, it would all be a matter of routine. Man against nature, competing in a fierce but clean battle.

The tall Colonel yawned contentedly and, leaning over, blew out the candle. The igloo glowed a dull silver in the sudden darkness.

'It's gone out, Captain,' said one of the men lying in the freezing snow.

'And about time,' Popvic muttered, surveying the little camp clearly outlined in the cold silver of the moon. The Fritzes had built their shelters in a tight little circle, covering at the most a hundred square metres of snowfield. Nice and compact, he told himself. And not a sentry in sight. 'They've already made their graves,' he said aloud, indicating the tomb-like igloos. 'All we've got to do is to bury them.'

No one laughed. The partisans were too cold and too weary, and perhaps a little afraid. There was something uncanny about the fact that in this remote little camp men lay sleeping peacefully, unaware of their fate.

Popvic shrugged and rose cautiously to his feet. Then he gave a hand signal. Like timber wolves the partisans advanced on the sleeping camp, coming in from all sides so that there would be no escape for the Germans once the shooting broke out.

One hundred and fifty metres . . . one hundred . . . seventy-five . . . Every detail of the little camp, down to the tin mess-tin filled with ice which hung from a stick outside one of the igloos, was clearly revealed in the moonlight. Somewhere someone was snoring loudly. Now nothing could go wrong, Popvic told himself, drawing his pistol and clicking off the safety catch with his thumb.

He had told his men to select an igloo, poke their weapons through the opening and fire. No one was to take unnecessary risks. Shoot first and ask questions afterwards – that was to be their motto. They would deal with the wounded Fritzes after they had broken their resistance. Not that Popvic expected any resistance. This night's work was going to be nothing but a massacre. *The Fritzes must not escape!*

Fifty metres to go. Now the men were treading more carefully, raising their feet and placing them down gingerly, as if they were walking over eggs. They were so close now that the slightest noise might give away their presence.

Forty metres.

He would keep one prisoner, Popvic promised himself, to help solve the mystery of what the Fritzes were doing in the remote mountains, where there were no military objectives. He'd take the man to Tito personally and let him tell the Comrade Marshal his story himself. In spite of the tension and biting cold, he smiled pleasantly to himself. Perhaps his success would persuade Tito not to have him shot in the post-war purges after all.

Thirty metres now.

Squatting behind the boulder overlooking the camp, his face contorted with hatred as well as fear, the Sergeant raised his sniper's rifle. His mind made up, he flashed it round until Popvic's back slid into the circle of glass. The Captain made a perfect target as he stood there, about to order the *attack.*

He knew that he *had* to kill Popvic. He had lost face with the men – they knew him now for what he was – and had always been – a coward, who had hidden away at HQ ever since the struggle had begun and who had been forced to go to the Front only when the reserves of able-bodied men had given out. Moreover, Popvic, the dandified swine, would undoubtedly instigate a court-martial once they returned. The pig would show him, a Party member, no mercy. Everybody knew at HQ that Popvic hated the Party with a passion; he fought not for the Cause but for the thrill of battle.

Slowly, his forefinger curled around the trigger. Popvic must die, and no one in the partisan band must escape. He would be the sole survivor. Tito would ensure that he was never sent to the Front again.

'ATT —

The heavy midnight silence was broken by a single sharp crack. The word died on Popvic's lips as he was struck by a tremendous blow in the small of his back. Abruptly, he was sitting foolishly in the snow, his pistol hanging in nerveless fingers, while all around him there were shouts, cries, the sudden hectic hammering of a machine-gun. Why were they firing? he asked himself. 'Mustn't fire yet,' he croaked, blood running out of the side of his mouth. 'Achieve surprise.'

He tried to get up, but his body would no longer obey him. Dropping his pistol, he tried to lever himself up with his arms, but they gave way beneath him. He fell heavily, flat on his face in the snow.

Once more he attempted to rise and then let his face to the blood-stained snow, whimpering like a little lost child. The next moment a burst of Tommy gun fire shattered the back of his skull. Two hundred yards away his murderer was running for his life down the mountainside, away from the massacre of his comrades, who were now caught completely exposed in the open . . .

THREE

'*Shoot him!*' Greul ordered drily, holding his smoking machine-pistol in his hands.

Ox-Jo looked up at the CO, who did not seem to notice the cold even though he was jacketless and barefoot.

Stuermer nodded.

With the muzzle of his Tommy gun, Ox-Jo forced the wounded partisan's head round. The prisoner stared up at him in the moonlight, his eyes filled with dumb animal patience. The big Bavarian clicked over to 'single' and pressed the trigger. The wounded man's head shattered under the impact. He died instantly.

Stuermer turned away hastily. The dream was over. They would never get away from this slaughter. Behind him Ox-Jo stamped over to the next wounded partisan, who lay groaning in the snow, his leg half-severed by a burst from one of the troopers. After a single shot, his groans ended.

Stuermer clenched his frozen fists in despair. *Would the killing never stop?*

Greul walked over to him. 'What now, sir?'

Stuermer forced himself to ask, 'What do you mean?'

'One of them got away. I saw him running down the slope with my own eyes. Besides –' he indicated the dead radio operator, his heavy apparatus still attached to his back – 'they had a radio.'

'You mean they either already know or will soon know that we are up here in the mountains, Greul?'

'Exactly, sir. This time the balloon has really gone up.'

Stuermer nodded grimly. 'You're right, Greul. Now they'll really be looking for us.' He forced himself to be businesslike. 'Sergeant-Major,' he bellowed, 'round the men up and let's get them on their way. There'll be no more sleep this night.'

Even Greul was aghast. 'You don't mean we're going to tackle the glacier tonight?'

'With a bit of luck the moonlight will hold up long enough for us to cross it. We'll rope up, of course.'

'But what if it doesn't – the moon I mean?' Greul objected. 'It would be suicide to attempt that kind of a climb in darkness, sir.'

'It's going to be suicide staying down here, too, Greul. We can expect more partisans by dawn. Come on now.'

'That's right, lads,' Ox-Jo was bellowing happily, his two hours of sleep having refreshed him, 'Let's hit that shitting asphalt now!'

In his igloo Stuermer prayed as he started to pull on his climbing boots. Time was running out.

Stuermer was already roped up. Impatiently he waited till the others did the same. The snow glittered like diamonds in the bright moonlight and there was no sound save the quick breathing of the busy troopers and the faint hiss as the wind moved the surface of the snow. For a moment Stuermer was overwhelmed by a sense of his own smallness and impotency in the face of the majesty and power of nature this beautiful, bright night. Then he concentrated on the task ahead, surveying the glacier, searching for signs of trouble.

They would zig-zag up the glacier-face, he decided, avoiding places covered with snow. He preferred the naked ice, for there could be deep crevices, folds, anything hidden under the snow.

'All roped up and ready to go, sir,' Ox-Jo reported, his breath fogging in the icy night air like a small grey cloud.

'Thank you, Ox,' Stuermer acknowledged. 'Get roped up yourself and bring up the rear – and keep a weather eye open for anything.'

'Yessir. I'll let you know if I see any naked blondes running around.'

'Be off with you, you rogue!' Stuermer raised his right

arm and brought it down with a gesture of finality. He stepped onto the glacier. 'Let's go!'

In a long line, each man roped five metres away from his neighbours, they started to plod up the steep slope. Their nailed boots bit into the ice, making a harsh, squeaking noise, as they moved with their bodies bent to take the strain and keep them balanced. Like flies crawling up the gleaming silver envelope of some monstrous zeppelin, they commenced the ascent, while the moon looked down on them with cruel detachment.

'Stay there you bastard, *stay*!' Ox-Jo, bringing up the rear, cursed.

'Don't let us down – here.'

It was now three o'clock. They had been climbing for nearly two hours and Stuermer could tell from the laboured breathing behind him that his sorely tried troopers were beginning to tire again. But he did not dare stop. He'd give the moon another hour perhaps before it disappeared – dawn came early in this region in May – and they had still another thousand metres to cover before they cleared the glacier.

He lowered his head again to try to avoid the full impact of the biting cold that had him continually blinking back tears. He started zig-zagging again, using the entrenching tool as a kind of ice-axe, and soon the backs of his legs screamed out in pain from bending his body at that unnatural angle. With infinite slowness the troopers followed their leader, edging their way across another fifty or so metres, before Stuermer changed direction again. Step by step they worked their way ever upwards, their faces crimson from the effort and the wind.

More than once Stuermer looked back. It seemed to him that they were hardly moving, so vast was the surface of the glacier. 'Keep going, will you,' he snarled each time. 'We've got to reach that summit soon.'

And then the silver light started to fade. Stuermer paused

in mid-stride, his breathing harsh and fast, and looked up. A dark cloud was beginning to cross the face of the moon.

No! he cursed. The men stumbled to a halt on the ice behind him. More clouds. Slowly, they started to blot out the light which had guided them this far.

Greul looked at the Colonel as the light faded rapidly.

Stuermer's voice, steady but unusually harsh, echoed strangely in that remote vast place, 'We go on.'

They marched upwards in virtually total darkness, with every man knowing the blind was leading the blind.

Stuermer was no longer cold, in spite of the icy wind which swept the face of the mountain, drawing its freezing cold from the glacier. His body dripped with the sweat of tension and fear. In the darkness he had led them onto a patch where a thin layer of snow covered the ice, hiding any danger that might lurk there from him. They were advancing at a snail's pace, while Stuermer probed every fresh step with the tip of his entrenching tool, racked with the agony of decision – *What lay below?* – every time he could not feel ice beneath the layer of snow.

Once he blundered into a group of snow-covered ice boulders which had him and his men, hearts thumping with sudden panic, sliding about. Twice he took his life into his hands: when he discovered that their progress was barred by ice fissures beneath the snow, he had jumped across them, praying fervently that the hidden ice on the other side would be firm enough to hold his weight. It had held.

Time passed with leaden feet. Stuermer kept glancing upwards but the moon was still completely hidden. And there was as yet no light on the horizon to the east, to indicate the dawn. They crept on.

About five o'clock, while Stuermer was working his way through another patch of snow in which he had blundered in the pitch-darkness, it happened. Completely without warning, the ground disappeared beneath him as his feet went through the thin layer of snow. His entrenching tool flew out of his hand. Involuntarily, taken totally by surprise, he screamed as he plunged down at a tremendous speed into nothingness!

For one long moment, Colonel Stuermer thought he was falling to his death. As the rope cut into his stomach cruelly, he gasped, all breath knocked out of him. But his dive did not end. He was still falling. Another jerk caused him to gasp out loud. Then his descent slowed down and stopped altogether, leaving him hanging in the freezing darkness, panting harshly, his body burning with pain from being knocked against the rocks during his fall.

Colonel Stuermer did not move: in shock, he could not. Then he pulled himself together with an effort of will and tried to reason out what had happened. The second jerk on the rope, which had finally stopped his downwards plunge, indicated that someone else had gone into the fissure, too. That meant there were two of them trapped. It meant, too, that the strain on the rope was doubled. Would it hold?

He forgot the other man. The pressure of the rope cutting cruelly into his waist was fast becoming unbearable. He could not breathe. If he did not relieve the pressure soon, it would cut off his air supply and he would black out. That would be fatal. Thanking God that he was carrying his Prusik sling and that it had not been wrenched from his belt during the fall, he forced his right foot into it, thus taking the pressure from his waist. Then he took a deep breath of icy air; it sliced into his lungs, but he was grateful for it all the same.

Somewhere above in the darkness, a disembodied voice called, 'Sir!' It seemed a long way off, but Stuermer recognized it. It was Greul's.

'All right! I'm alive!' he said in a cracked voice which he hardly recognized as his own.

'Thank God for that!' Greul said fervently.

'What's the situation up there?'

'One of the guides, the one with the crossed eyes, went

over with you. We can't see a damn thing, Colonel, but we think, to judge by the length of rope up here, he must be five metres or so down.'

'Did the rope break on the surface?' Stuermer asked, making a quick calculation. He was still attached to the guide, so that would mean five and five metres – say, twelve altogether. He was twelve metres from the entrance to the fissure.

'Yessir.'

'Is he unconscious?'

'We think so, sir.' Greul replied. 'He hasn't responded.'

Stuermer made a quick decision, praying that Cockeye was only knocked out and had no broken bones. He knew he must get out of the freezing hole while he could still work his limbs. 'Nobody is to attempt to come down,' he ordered.

'But —'

'No, buts, Greul,' Stuermer cut in with as much firmness as he could muster, for now his teeth were beginning to chatter. 'I'll climb up to him. We're still attached. Once I reach the surface (*if*, a little voice inside him said cynically), you can use that rope to pull him out. Now no more talk.'

'Good luck, sir,' Greul said, but Stuermer was no longer listening. He was already beginning the climb.

Like all fissures he had known, this one would be broad at the bottom, narrow at the top. They always damned well were. He would not even bother to attempt to find the rock-wall to give himself some kind of leverage. It would be wasted effort. He would have to pull himself up, hoping desperately that the stout rope, would not break again.

In total darkness, the only sound to be heard in that eerie, freezing chimney being his own laboured breathing, Colonel Stuermer fought a lone battle against nature, hauling himself up the make-shift ladder made of the sling and the rope itself. The muscles of his arms and legs blazed from the strain and he felt the strength ebb from his lean body as the cold crowded in, squeezing it out of him, making him consider wanting to surrender to its icy grip and drift into the bliss of oblivion.

Stuermer fought back desperately, the strain on the rope forgotten now as he worked himself up millimetre by millimetre. Suddenly his head bumped into something. Rock? No, it moved and he could feel small, hard objects press through his matted hair into the flesh of his scalp. Nails! He was directly underneath the unconscious guide. That meant he had only another five or six metres to go. His heart leapt with joy.

The fissure was narrower here, as he had guessed it would be. He began to squeeze upwards alongside the unconscious man, who seemed to be suspended in mid-air! the body swayed each time Stuermer touched it in his ascent. First the ankles, then the knees, the waist. The man's chest. Stuermer's distended nostils and wide-open mouth were assailed by the heavy strench of garlic that enimated from the unconscious guide. Involuntarily, he turned his head to one side.

The hasty moved proved fatal. There was a sharp crack as the rope broke under the strain. The sling went too. In one frightening flash, he had lost all support.

Stuermer grabbed at the unconscious man. The two of them twirled in a crazy dance as the section of rope which held Cockeye, obviously attached to some rock outcrop, sang out under the strain of the new load.

Stuermer fought to subdue his panic. The rope could not hold both of them much longer. Trying to control the wild whirling movement, he thrust one boot out tentatively. '*Thank God!*' he croaked when it struck rock, while Cockeye groaned in his arms. He pushed out another boot. Now his body was bent in a U-shape; his arms were clasped around Cockeye, his feet pushed squarely against the rock-face. From above there was the hissing sound which usually indicated that the pressure on the rope was beginning to become excessive. He had seconds left. He must take a chance.

Letting go, Stuermer thrust out his arms backwards, like

a champion diver diving backwards from the board. For one frightening moment, he felt nothing and imagined himself already plummeting to the floor of the fissure far below. Then his two hands slapped into the rock and he could feel it cutting into them savagely, drawing blood.

But that did not matter now. This seemed to him the happiest moment of his life. He had done it!

He was stuck there with the swinging man nudging gently against his right side. His body was suspended horizontally, his spine arched, supported by his bleeding hands and boots. The next step was to turn round. He could not chance trying to get his shoulders against the rock-face and working his way upwards to the exit that way. It would be too risky.

Gingerly he began to worm himself round, feeling the rock dig deeper into his torn palms. Under other circumstances, he knew, he would have found the situation absurd: here he was, one of the world's greatest climbers, attempting a move that was laughably clumsy and for which there was no precedent in the climbing textbooks. But in this eerie crack in the rock, all alone save the unconscious guide, he took it deadly seriously. Then he had done it and he was facing downwards.

He knew he must take one final chance. Placing his left hand against the surface of the rock, fingers spread to give him some support, he let go with his right hand. Carefully he smoothed his hand outwards. Slowly, sweat oozing from every pore, he ran his hand down the rough surface of the rock, trying to locate a hold.

Then he found it. A vertical crack. His heart leapt joyfully. He inserted his fingers into it. They went in as far as the knuckles but no more. It would have to be enough.

He crooked his right arm, tensed and counted up to three. Then he let go with his feet. They thudded against the opposite wall, leaving his right shoulder bearing the entire weight of his body. His muscles screamed under the strain. Biting his teeth into his bottom lip, he heaved; his left hand sought a hold and found it. He was moving upwards again. Opposite him the guide groaned, he was coming to.

Stuermer reached up farther. Another metre. Then his searching, bleeding fingers found a knotted rope, tangled around an outcrop of rock. Supported by one hand and his foothold, he undid the knots with trembling fingers and took the jagged end between his teeth. He climbed on, tugging it with him.

Suddenly a dim blur loomed up in front of him. A face! He had reached the exit. The next moment eager hands were hauling him up and out. He lay gasping in the snow, bruised, ashen-face, trembling, his heart pounding away furiously, but triumphant!

Two hours later, the first rays of the blood-red ball of the sun cleared the snow-capped peaks. Warmed by its rays, the men of Edelweiss Stormtroop overcame the terrible glacier.

When, finally, Stuermer ordered a halt, the troopers collapsed exhausted on the frozen snow. With Greul and Conk, the Colonel climbed wearily to the look-out spot on the summit and stared northwards where range after range spread out like a relief map in front of them, buried under the snow, which sparkled crimson in the ascending sun.

Conk wiped a dewdrop from his long, red, dripping nose and pointed to the east. 'To Potok,' he announced. He gestured to the west. 'Kazanci,' he said.

'Then Dvrar must be in that direction,' Greul said, indicating north-west.

Conk nodded. 'Perhaps twenty–thirty kilometres across mountains. As crow fly.'

Greul's lean, bearded face hardened and his eyes sparkled with a trace of his usual fanaticism. 'Then we're almost there! Forty-eight hours more and we'll have him!'

Stuermer nodded wearily. *Tito.* But his heart was not in this mission. The final result of all this effort would undoubtedly be more bloodshed. He waved a limp hand at his men. 'All right, let's get started again. We've got to get down into the valley before the reconnaissance planes start looking for us.'

Like a bunch of aged asthmatics, Germany's finest military climbers began their infinitely weary progress down the mountain, on the last stage of their journey.

FOUR

'Comrades,' Tito said, cool and businesslike, 'I believe there is no need for me to go into the general tactical picture in any detail.' He gestured at the map. 'Our troops on the Western Flank are withdrawing from Bihac in the north to Lapac until they reach the line of the River Una, which I have ordered them to hold.'

'It's very close to Drvar, Comrade Marshal,' Jovanovic said, his pale intelligent face worried.

'I know, I know. But I think the Fritzes will never reach the Una.' He caught the light of hope in their eyes and held up his hand hurriedly, the fingers outspread, almost as if he wished physically to push back their relief.

'Don't misunderstand me. I still think the attack on the Western Flank is a feint. Chief-of-Staff, tell them why.'

Jovanovic stepped forward. 'We have received a report from agents in the Zagreb area that the Fritzes are massing nearly one hundred gliders at their local emergency field.'

Someone whistled low in surprise. Another officer gasped. An excited discussion broke out but urgently Jovanovic held up his nicotine-stained hands to silence it.

'Comrades,' he commanded, 'silence please.' He faced Tito. 'With all due respect, I do not think we have to fear an airborne landing, in spite of the gliders. I am one hundred percent convinced that the enemy will attack by land. You might be right that the present attack is a trick, a blind to fool us, but German troop concentrations here at Kulen – Vakuf – Knin —' he slapped the map with his knuckles as he mentioned each name – 'Jecero – all indicate a full-scale offensive – *by land*!' He emphasized the words and stared at his superior almost challengingly.

Tito frowned. One day, Jovanovic, he told himself, I'll have your sly head. But now he concentrated on the problem on hand. 'All right, I will grant you that these reports of troop concentrations come from some of the most reliable agents. But so does the one from Zagreb. So how do you explain the gliders, eh?' He poked a stubby forefinger at his Chief-of-Staff.

Before he could answer that weighty question, the door was flung open behind them without ceremony. Cold air flooded the overheated, smoke-filled map room.

A tall, sparse, excited figure stood in the doorway, face gleaming excitedly. It was the Englishman, the head of their mission, wearing that absurd skirt, he affected. '*Dosvedanya, tovarischi,*' he called in his heavily-accented Russian.

Tito's anger vanished. McLean was the stereotyped polite Englishman, even though he was a capitalist. He would not burst into a room unless he had something important to report. 'What is it, Colonel?' he asked, while Jovanovic, the Stalinist, watched the two of them carefully, as usual suspicious whenever Tito had dealings with the English Military Mission.

'I have good news for you, Marshal,' McLean replied. 'We have just received a signal from Italy reporting that the RAF has plastered Zagreb field. The gliders there have been totally destroyed.'

The Chief-of-Staff's look of suspicion vanished, and all around him the staff officers gave a sigh of relief. 'What did I tell you, Comrade Marshal?' Jovanovic said enthusiastically. 'Whatever the German plans were for those gliders, they are destroyed now.' He clicked to attention with abrupt formality. 'Comrade, I must report that the unified opinion of the High Command is this. In the next few days we can expect a full-scale German attack by land.'

Tito gave in, although his intuition told him that Jovanovic was not completely right. That sense of thick air still troubled him, but he knew he could not casually overrule the High Command of the National Liberation Army. It would destroy the troops' confidence. Besides, what could he offer as an alternative? Just vague suspicions, born of a lifetime of clandestine work where nothing had been clear-cut and tangible. He let it pass without further argument. 'All right, comrades, I'm sure you're right. Please don't let me disturb you any more. Get on with your planning.'

He turned to McLean and took him by the arm, ignoring Jovanovic, who was still watching him. Amicably, he escorted him to the door. Outside the Stukas were hurling themselves out of the hard blue sky once more, hurtling down, their sirens howling hysterically, as if their pilots might not be able to pull them out of the crazy dive.

Tito ignored the racket. It had been going on so long now he had become used to it. 'In two days, Colonel,' he announced, looking up at the tall, skinny Englishman, 'I shall give a little party to celebrate my fifty-second birthday, which takes place on the 25th of May. I would like you and your second-in-command to join me for a drink.'

McLean flashed his professional smile, acquired during his pre-war Foreign Office training, although he knew and dreaded the long, drunken partisan orgies which grew from a casual invitation to have a little drink. 'Will there be whisky?' he asked carefuly.

Tito grinned. 'Yes, my dear Colonel. You won't be forced to drink our plum brandy. There will be whisky for you Englishmen.'

McLean was embarrassed. 'I didn't mean —'

Tito cut him short. 'Be off now and watch out for those damned dive-bombers.'

'Thank you, Marshal. I will.' McLean hurried across the debris-littered street towards his waiting jeep, as the Stukas came howling in once more. Tito waited till it had started to draw away; then he went back inside to the hectic activity of the Citadel once more.

Tito, once called Broz and many other names since then, had exactly seventy-two hours left before he was due to die in the same mysterious way that he had lived . . .

BOOK FIVE: OPERATION KNIGHT'S MOVE

ONE

In a great V that stretched for over two kilometres the Junkers carrying the 500th SS Parachute Battalion flew over the mountains. That afternoon the order had arrived at battalion HQ: *Commence Operation Knight's Move* – using the code-name for the great attack on the partisan HQ. Two hours of hectic activity had followed: loading the waiting planes, making a last minute check of weapons and equipment, filling the tanks of the aircraft with fuel. Now they were airborne, the tough SS paras in their bulky overalls, bursting with ammunition, food, flasks of drink, buried in their own thoughts, silent and pensive. Even the veteran *skat* players at the back of each plane had grown silent, forgetting the card game.

Behind them in the second wave came the gliders, their skids wrapped in thick rolls of barbed wire to reduce their braking distance. Most of the men they carried, clad in the thick rubber knee pads and rubber helmets to absorb the impact as they hit the deck, were already sharpening their knives, which they would use to rip open the thin canvas of the DO 232s once they landed.

Below, the halftracks of Captain Attila's *Prinz Eugen* volunteers rattled through the night, their decks heavy with snoring SS men clad in their mottled camouflaged suits, while in the cab of the leading halftrack, Attila, as cynical and contemptuous as ever, smoked his black cheroot, his one eye searching the night scene for the least sign of trouble.

All along the German front, troops were on the move, telephones rang in HQs, despatch-drivers raced through the night, officers issued orders, while in their map rooms the staff, drinking cup after cup of ersatz coffee, waited tensely for the first news from the Front.

It was nearly four o'clock in the morning. Soon it would

be dawn. In the para-transports the red warning lights began to glow. The dispatchers wove their way down the cramped planes and opened the doors, letting icy air in, making those who had tried to sleep cry out angrily at the disturbance.

Further back the gliders swung into battle formation.

'Cast off!' came the order.

The pilots towing the gliders released their cables. After a slight jerk the glider pilots brought up the noses of their wooden planes, so that they would not loose height immediately. Now the Junkers transports banked in a slow curve, making for their home fields. All of a sudden all noise had ceased. The gliders sailed on silently. Everything on this May dawn seemed unbelievably calm and peaceful.

'Stop!' Attila commanded.

They had reached the starting-line. The long column of halftracks rattled to a halt. The sleeping grenadiers awoke and started to urinate over the sides of the vehicles causing the frozen dust to hiss. Others shielded matches in their cupped hands and lit their first cigarette of the day.

Slowly and without intending to swagger, Captain Attila walked up the road, knowing as did his watching men that the enemy positions were only five hundred metres away. He focussed his night-glasses. Nothing. The partisans of the First Proletarian Division occupying the heights ahead showed no sign that they had heard the halftracks' approach. There might well be no one there. The line was silent. The partisans slept on.

From the sea now, two waves of bombers – Heinkels III and Junkers 88 – started to zoom in, to avoid the partisan flak which was known to be particularly strong around Drvar. They would lay a carpet of bombs all along the route taken by the airborne force and confuse the enemy flak; then they would turn their attention on the HQ itself, bombing it until the para-transports were but a few kilometres away.

Operation Knight's Move was going according to plan.

*

'Oh, my sainted godfather,' Colonel McLean said to no one in particular, slapping his forehead in mock wonder. 'What the damn next?' He almost upset his fifth whisky of the night in his surprise – and whisky was at a premium in partisan territory.

They had been celebrating the eve of the Marshal's birthday for hours now and black-out regulations had long been forgotten. Fires burnt everywhere and more than once, enthusiastic drunken partisans had fired star shells into the night, an expensive kind of fireworks display. Drunken, excited civilians, the women mostly in traditional costume, were everywhere drinking, shouting and singing. Twice he and the Chief-of-Staff had warned the Marshal he'd better go back to the caves in case the fires attracted the attention of German night-bombers. But, his face flushed red from drink and an enormous cigar stuck in his little pipe-holder, he had refused.

'*Nastrovya!*' he had toasted McLean wildly in Russian. On the second toast, he had placed his arm affectionately around the worried Englishman's shoulder and had begun a spirited recital of the *Owl and the Pussy-Cat* in heavily accented but passable English. McLean had not known that Tito spoke his own language.

And hand in hand, on the edge of the sand,
They danced in the light of the moon.

Concluding the verse, Tito had winked at the taller man in a conspiratorial fashion. 'You not know I speak English, eh?' he had remarked.

Now the party had reached its highpoint, and both partisans and drunken civilians were parading through the streets, singing and shouting, bearing burning pitch-torches so that a worried McLean could not help thinking the Germans must be able to see them from as far away as Belgrade.

It did not seem to worry the partisan leader. Standing on the balcony of the house next to the Citadel, dressed in his new Marshal's uniform, he waved his cigar at them and accepted their cheers and the ever repeated choruses of '*Long Live Tito! Long Live the National Liberation Army! Long Live the United Peoples of Jugoslavia!* in the manner born. McLean could not help thinking Churchill could not have pulled it off any better.

Captain Ryska, Commander of the 500th SS Parachute Battalion, positioned himself at the door of the Junkers 52. The icy wind whipped at his overalls. The Junkers were now at an altitude of about 200 metres. The combat-experienced para captain knew it was low for jumping, but they would not be much endangered by enemy flak at this height, although they ran the risk of broken bones and twisted ankles.

'Get ready!' the despatcher bellowed above the roar of the engines. 'Two minutes to go!'

Holding on tightly with one hand, he checked the front of his equipment. Behind him his number two did the same. All along the line, the tense, pale-faced paras followed suit. This was the moment of truth.

At the side of the door the green light winked urgently.

'*Go!*' the despatcher cried, slapping his hand down hard on the Captain's back.

The Captain launched himself forward immediately. The weight of his pack and chute seemed to snatch him out of the plane like an invisible hand. He began to drop to the ground at a terrifying speed. *Crack!* After a hefty tug beneath his armpits, the great white cloud of parachute blossomed forth above him, breaking his fall. He started to drift downwards while, above him, in the unreal light of the new dawn, man after man fell out of the slow transports.

'Prepare for landing!' The order broke the tense silence in the gliders.

Routinely, the soldiers raised their legs from the floor, braced their arms underneath and waited. Up front the glider pilots sweated as they prepared to land in the semi-darkness. The hiss of the wind against the canvas fuselage grew louder. Somewhere far away there was the rattle of a machine-gun, clearly audible over the noise of the wind. The ground raced up to meet the gliders. At the very last moment the pilots jerked up the planes' noses. Two thousand pounds of man and material hit the earth with rending crash, tearing of canvas, squeals of protesting wood.

The barbed wire wrapped around the skids to shorten the sliding distance snapped like string. In a high wake of dust, the first one skidded to a stop. One by one they landed, then the men inside began cutting their way out of the sides instead of bursting out through the doors to face the machine-guns waiting for them.

Attila could wait no longer. Tossing away his cigar, '*Roll em!*' he bellowed.

Motor after motor roared into ear-splitting activity.

Attila swung himself into the cab of the first one and thrust down the windscreen, levelling his machine-pistol over it. 'All right, driver,' he cried to the pale-faced kid driving, 'finger out. Let's go!'

On the horizon where the partisan line was located, flares started to rise in crazy profusion. Attila grinned to himself. The Jugs had been caught with their knickers down. Perhaps this time they were going to pull it off altogether and kill the buggers?

The vehicles roared forward, while slugs howled off their metal sides harmlessly, as if nothing and nobody could stop them now.

The telephone shrilled in the duty officer's room in the Citadel. Lieutenant Cartat, the duty officer, cursed. Down below one of the local girls carrying a torch in the procession was wearing a very low-cut dress. At that angle he could almost see what she had eaten for supper. He strode to the phone and picked it up, growling, 'Duty officer here!'

'Here the Sixth Brigade,' an excited voice at the other end shouted, forcing him to take his ear away from the phone a little.

'All right . . . all right, I can hear you. Can't you keep it down to a dull roar?'

'Planes everywhere,' the unknown voice said. 'Paras landing everywhere in Sixth Brigade area.'

'*What?*' Cartat exploded. 'Are you drunk, man?'

'I wish I were, comrade. Now tell the High Command, at the double. They're coming in the—'

A sudden click and the phone went dead in the shocked officer's hand.

The impossible had happened. Drvar was being attacked from the air!

TWO

'*Avioni!*'

The partisan standing next to the church bells mounted on a scaffolding and positioned on the hill overlooking Drvar started to ring the hundredweight bells with all his strength, his eyes growing wider as plane after plane came into sight. In two great V's, the silver birds were sweeping in to destroy the town below. Then he dropped the rope and ran for his life as the first bomb started to howl down on the hilltop position.

The urgent tolling of the looted church bells broke into the young duty officer's excited explanation of what he had heard from the Sixth Brigade. Jovanovic, his drunkenness vanished immediately, listened silently, concerned and disbelieving, while all around him orderlies ran back and forth in the Citadel placing important papers into fire-proof containers – standard practice – and telephones jingled urgently.

To his right, a frustrated staff officer was bellowing angrily into the phone. 'But I tell you, operator, you've got to raise the First Proletarian Division. You've got to! It'll cost me my head if you don't!'

'And what else did the Sixth say?' Jovanovic demanded.

'Nothing. The line just went dead.'

'A provocation? A drunk?' the Chief-of-Staff said urgently, not wanting to believe that he had failed in his assessment of the German ability to launch an airborne attack because he had been blinded by his own prejudices.

'It didn't sound like that to —'

The rest of the young officer's words were drowned by the first thick, stomach-turning salvo of bombs. The Citadel rocked like a ship at sea suddenly caught in a violent storm. Plaster tumbled down from the ceiling in a dense grey, choking rain. Somewhere a window shattered and a man screamed piteously. Involuntarily, Jovanovic flashed a glance out of the upper-storey window.

A partisan had been guillotined by a huge piece of broken glass, which had sliced his head neatly from his shoulders. For one long horrifying moment he tottered there, hands raised as if he were groping at the awful emptiness, trying to locate the missing head which was now rolling away down the swaying street like a bearded football. With a final convulsive shudder, the headless torso jetted blood in thick scarlet streams onto the cobblestones.

Forcing back the bitter bile which had risen to his throat threatening to choke him, the Chief-of-Staff swung round, ignoring the shaking building and the pale faces all around him. Outside the rattles sounded, whistles were being blown and a half a score voices called, 'Alarm! . . . *Alarm!* . . . *Alarm!*' He could hear the sound of heavy boots stamping down the street, heading for the shelters.

'Wake him – the Marshal! He's just gone to bed, but wake him. Bring him down here at once. Understood?'

'Understood, comrade.' The Lieutenant swung round and pushed his way through the excited throng at the door.

Jovanovic strode to the Major trying to raise the First Division. He tugged the phone from his hand brutally. 'Operator, here the Chief-of-Staff. If I don't have the First within the minute you are a dead man.'

He waited, a thousand and one ideas racing through his head. He was frightened but it was not occasioned by the present emergency. His concern lay two thousand kilometres away in Moscow. In the Kremlin. If anything happened to Tito, Stalin would have his head. That was one of his two functions here – sometimes he thought it was his most important one – to be Tito's watch-dog. He had been appointed by Stalin personally, to ensure that the obstinate partisan leader always toed the Soviet line, for when the victory was won, there was not to be an independent Jugoslavia as Tito fondly believed there would be. Jugoslavia would be firmly within the Soviet sphere of influence.

The operator's frightened voice broke into his reverie. 'The First Partisan Division, Comrade General!'

'Polje.' It was the commander of the 1st personally speaking, his voice cracked and just barely under control.

'Jovanovic! What can you do —'

Polje cut him shortly abruptly. 'We are being subjected to very heavy attack up here. The Fritzes are attacking with armoured units from the direction of Bihac, Jajce, heading for Drvar. Our screen and forward units have already been overrun. It's that damned SS Division again – the *Prinz Eugen*. My men are no match for them —'

Now it was Jovanovic's turn to interrupt, his voice harsh and resolute. '*Hold them!*' he commanded, above the whistle and roar of the bomb outside. 'You must stop them, do you understand? If you can't counter-attack to the front, hit them in the flank. Blow up all bridges. Put out landmines. Get your best snipers at all key points. *But stop them!*'

'But I've done all that already, Comrade Jovanovic. It's not enough.'

'Why not?'

'Because they are already landing paratroopers and glider-borne troops way behind our line, not far from Drvar itself.'

The Chief-of-Staff's heart sank. Again, confirmation that he had made – perhaps – a fatal mistake. He swayed and grabbed hold of the table, then pulled himself together. 'All right, Comrade General, I understand. Do your best to hold back the main advance, but detach two brigades. March them immediately to Drvar. I've got nothing more than a half a battalion up here.'

'It will be done!' Polje answered, but there was no confidence in his voice. The phone went dead in Jovanovic's trembling hand.

'Who was that?'

The Chief-of-Staff swung round. It was Tito, his eyes behind the gold-rimmed glasses red from lack of sleep, his splendid marshal's uniform of the night abandoned for rough mountain clothes devoid of any badge of rank.

'Polje of the First. He's under heavy attack from the *Prinz Eugen.* He says that paras and gliderborne troops have dropped to his rear.' Jovanovic swallowed hard. 'But I can hardly believe it.'

For a moment oppressive silence prevailed inside the Citadel, while outside the bombs continued to drop as the Heinkels and Junkers zoomed down at tree-top height, confident now that they had knocked out the partisan flak on the hills outside the burning town.

Tito considered the situation quickly. For the defence of the town he had assigned 350 men of his guard battalion, divided into four troops: three armed with infantry weapons, the fourth manning the now silent flak cannon. Not very much to hold back the elite German troops.

'Get the three troop commanders in here,' he said decisively, breaking the silence. 'Bring up those Italian tanks of ours. They'll be useful against the paras – they'll have no heavy weapons . . .'

Order after order was rapped out, while the telephones started to jingle again and flustered staff officers marked every new German identification on the big map.

The three young officers came running in and stopped short when they saw Tito's back.

The Chief-of-Staff strode over to them with more firmness than he felt. 'You will fight to the last bullet – Drvar must be held!' His eyes flashed from one face to the other. They were filled with the keen desire for some desperate glory. He knew instinctively he could rely upon them. 'If your men fail to hold them back and the Fritzes capture Tito, that would mean the end of our long battle to liberate our country. Are you clear in your minds what that means?'

'Yes, Comrade General,' they snapped in unison, their eyes sparkling.

'Tito and the Party must survive. That is the only thing which is important at this moment. We can stand a defeat, but we cannot stand the loss of Marshal Tito. *Tito must live!*' he cried.

'*Tito must live!*' they echoed, their voices full of desperate enthusiasm. Tito turned, eyes full of compassion and at the same time cynicism at the way his Chief-of-Staff was exploiting their youth. 'I shall need only one troop with me when I return to the caves.'

'God be thanked that you have made that decision, Comrade Marshal!' the Chief-of-Staff said. He had feared that Tito would insist on staying in Drvar.

'There is no God,' Tito said drily and then nodded at the taller of the three young officers. 'You will accompany as my bodyguard. The rest of you will remain here. I'll ensure that you'll get reinforcements —' he hesitated only a fraction of a second and then lied glibly – 'within the hour. All right, Lieutenant, let's be on our way.' Then, turning to Jovanovic, 'Well?'

'For a little while I shall stay behind here, trying to get things organized. I have made a serious error – I must attempt to rectify it. With a bit of luck I'll be able to join you in the caves in the next couple of hours or so.'

'As you wish,' Tito said, turning to his bodyguard. 'All right, young man, let's see you start earning your pay this fine May morning.'

Grinning almost happily, the three officers clattered out behind him into the burning morning.

The Chief-of-Staff turned back to his urgent task of getting the defences organized. 'Call the Officers' Training School. I want the Commander to bring his cadets,' he began to shout at one of the sweating telephone operators.

He never completed the order. A dirty, bedraggled figure with sergeant's stars on his shoulders staggered through the door crying 'General Jovanovic . . . Comrade General Jovanovic!'

In spite of the emergency, the Chief-of-Staff paused; the man's appearance was so striking, so desperate. 'You're Sergeant Matschurek, aren't you?' he said, recognizing the man. 'You were here at HQ before you were posted to Popvic's Eleventh.' Suddenly he realized that they hadn't heard from the cynical ex-Guards captain for over a week now. 'Where is Popvic?' he asked urgently. 'What has happened?'

Stammering the dishevelled man, who had shot Captain Popvic, gave his own version of the attack, emphasizing how he had been the only survivor in the battle between the Eleventh and the strange intruders; how he had attempted to rescue the dying captain but had been felled and knocked unconscious by a stray bullet before he had been able to do so. When he had re-awoken, the company had been wiped out and the enemy had disappeared, heading north in the general direction of Drvar.

'Are you sure?' the Chief-of-Staff demanded. 'Are you sure that they were heading north?'

Matschurek nodded, wondering as the bombs continued to whistle down outside whether he had not made a mistake coming back to HQ.

'But there are no reports whatsoever of enemy troops in that area!'

'They were mountaineers. Captain Popvic, who used to climb before the war, said that they must be. They'd take the mountains and avoid the valleys where our people are.'

'Exactly!' Jovanovic snapped his fingers excitedly. 'Exactly!' For a moment he forgot the stinking, trembling man opposite him. Already a vague idea of what the Fritzes were up to was beginning to form in his mind; also, the dangers it held for his future security. 'All right, grab a rifle and join one of the defence troops.'

'But I'm tired and hungry. I've been marching for nearly two days now, Comrade General,' the NCO quavered.

Jovanovic dismissed him angrily with a wave of his hand. 'Get on with it.' He turned, leaving the miserable wretch to slink out to the battle which awaited him, and strode to the nearest phone. 'Top priority!' he rasped to the operator.

'But it's a civilian number,' the distant operator protested in surprise.

'This is the Chief-of-Staff,' he barked. 'When I say top priority, I mean it. Now get that number!'

'At once, Commander General . . . at once.'

A few seconds later a soft voice answered at the other end, saying, 'Tomic. Tomic's Apothecary.'

Under any other circumstances, Jovanovic would have laughed: in the midst of desperate battle 'Tomic's Apothecary' seemed strangely out of place. But not at this particular moment.

'Tomic, this is Jovanovic. Drop everything and come over here immediately. I think at last I'm going to need your services.'

'At once, comrade.' Tomic answered. He hung up without question.

The Chief-of-Staff breathed out hard and prayed that the chemist had been practising the role Moscow had trained him for over so many months, although never wishing he would have to play it. Soon, possibly, everything might depend upon him . . .

And in the dingy little bedroom behind his shop, Tomic took off his shabby white coat, put on gold-rimmed spectacles (even though he had perfect vision) and then stared at himself in the fly-blown mirror, in the side of which was tucked a photograph of the Marshal. He was pleased with what he saw reflected there. *The man in the photo could have been his twin!*

THREE

A soft swish. The Tito column did not hear the new sound, while the thud-thud of the bombs behind them died away, until it was almost too late. Abruptly a large, green-camouflaged shape blocked out the view through the windscreen of Tito's jeep. Next instant it hushed in to land. There was grinding scream of air brakes and the howl of the protesting wooden fuselage. Tito hastily grabbed the wheel from the surprised young driver and swung the jeep straight into the left ditch.

'*What in God's name* —' began the Lieutenant behind him.

'*Glider!*' Tito yelled, dropping over the side of the smashed jeep. Tiggan yelped at his legs as he grabbed for his pistol and threw himself behind the nearest boulder.

Up ahead, the men of the point were dancing around the smashed glider. Dust was slowly beginning to settle on its silent shape.

'Get down, you fools!' Tito yelled. The peasant boys had obviously never seen a glider before. They thought it was an ordinary plane which had been shot down. In a moment he knew they would discover their mistake to their cost. '*DOWN!... DOWN!...*'

Too late! The Germans were already ripping open the thin canvas with their knives, firing as they exited. The surprised partisans fell down everywhere. Yelling in triumph, the Germans went to ground.

Tito cursed. The way to the cave seemed blocked.

A moment later, he knew he was right. Another glider was coming down. It hit the trail, slid frighteningly to the right, was caught just in time and then shuddered to a stop. The barbed wire around its skids burst like pistol shots under the strain.

'Fire!' the Lieutenant yelled wildly.

He rose to his feet, ignoring the bullets already winging on their way or howling off the boulder. He pressed the trigger of his Sten. The little English machine-pistol chattered in his hands and his first salvo caught the Germans as they burst out of the hanging door. They were thrown to all sides in screaming confusion. He changed his magazine hurriedly, then pressed the trigger and poured the whole magazine into them. Screaming and yelling at the tops of their voices, legs and arms flailing as they were hit over and over again, they dropped; the pile of their bodies blocked the door of the glider.

A potato-masher grenade came whirling through the air. The Lieutenant dropped just in time. The grenade exploded in a thick crump on the far side of the boulder. Shrapnel and slivers of red-hot metal flew everywhere.

Tito made his decision. The trail was blocked and they could not wait for the bodyguard troop to clear it. Perhaps new gliders were on the way. They had to get out now. 'Lieutenant, let's go!'

'Abandon the vehicles?'

'Yes, if you don't want to lose your life!' He started to crawl back to the rest of the column, stalled just behind the cover of the bend. 'All right, everybody out,' he yelled above the racket. 'You heard! Up in the hills – *at the double*!'

A minute later Tito, Jugoslavia's sole marshal, head of a quarter million-strong partisan army, was running for his life. Enemy bullets stitched a blue, angry pattern at his flying heels.

With a yell of triumph, the German gliderborne troops rose to their feet and began to follow, firing as they came.

Operation Knight's Move was getting off to a good start.

The SS paras started to push into the outskirts of the burning town. Even before the echoes of the last salvo of bombs had died away, they were already pelting towards the hastily erected partisan defences. A group of them skidded to a stop behind a wrecked outhouse. Trained to act quickly and efficiently, the man with the tube held it up at a 45-degree angle, while the second para fixed the tripod and base plate. Immediately he had finished, the third man of the crew thrust home the bomb, turned the firing wheel and fired.

Plop. The bomb landed squarely on the partisan central strongpoint. Their ancient Lewis machine-gun plus its two-man crew disappeared in a violet flash. The paras doubled forward once more, springing lightly over the bodies of their fallen comrades.

Another glider came sailing in, blazing as it crashed. It lay between the paras and the partisans, burning fiercely, incinerating its crew.

'Forward!' Captain Ryska ordered, taking advantage of the burning glider, no feeling in his voice for his dead comrades. Using the glider for cover, the men behind him dashed forward.

The partisans blazed away, trying to pick them off behind the flaming wall of the glider, but failed to find their targets. Next instant the Germans had broken down the door of the house to the right of the partisan line. They slaughtered the terrified civilian occupants with a swift burst and, trampling over their still heaving bodies, fled out into the main street beyond.

The SS paras had turned the first partisan line, neatly outflanking it, and now pelted down the burning, battle-torn street towards to the heart of the Drvar's defences – the Citadel.

Rendulic was excited. '*Hauptsturmführer!*' he cried, his voice metallic and distorted by the radio's static, 'the first news from the Five-hundredth Parachute Battalion is good. They had penetrated the outskirts of Drvar, and although the situation is confused, they are believed to be heading for the Citadel. When last seen the battalion CO and his Group Red were well on the way to that objective.'

'Good, sir,' Attila said dutifully and ducked as another partisan shell whizzed over the parked halftrack. 'Things are rather quiet here.' He grinned to himself and stared at the burning halftracks everywhere and the bodies of the partisans which littered the shell-holed ground ahead.

'I'm pleased to hear that,' Rendulic said, the irony wasted upon him. 'Because I want you to change the direction of your attack.'

'*Change?*'

'Yes. The SS paras seem to be able now to take care of themselves.' Even at this stage of the operation Rendulic was not giving away the fact that Operation Knight's Move was a gigantic, costly feint. Still, he knew it would not do any harm *now* to give Stuermer a little muscle in the form of *Prinz Eugen*'s armoured vehicles. 'I want you to change direction, taking the road that leads south-east out of Drvar towards the village of Batasi in the mountains, some six kilometres away.'

'What is to be my objective, sir?' Attila asked.

'You will be contacted,' Rendulic answered mysteriously. 'In two hours' time. Report your position then and I personally will give you further instructions.'

Attila shook his head. 'Well, one thing sir, I've been on plenty of ops in my time, but never on one where I was commanded by the Army Commander personally.'

'Over and out' was General Rendulic's only reply.

FOUR

'For God's sake, take off those damned glasses,' Jovanovic snapped angrily, 'and close the door!' Swiftly he reached inside the drawer of his desk and brought out a scarf. He flung it at Tomic. 'And wrap that around your chin. Do you want to give us away with that mug of yours?'

The chemist complied wordlessly, while the Chief-of-Staff buckled on his heavy pistol belt, complete with two English-made Mills bombs. While Tomic watched him in silence, he slapped his upper pockets, as if to check that they still contained whatever he kept there.

Outside the high-pitched German machine-gun hissed again and Tomic could hear the slap of the slugs as they ran the length of the Citadel. The Fritzes could not be more than two hundred metres away now. Soon they'd be in the courtyard below.

The Chief-of-Staff seemed to read his mind. 'We're pulling out in ten minutes,' he announced, slipping two maps in his leather case and slinging that over his shoulder, too. 'The two of us and a handful of trusted officers. The rest —' He shrugged cynically, leaving his sentence incomplete.

Tomic knew what he meant. The rest would be left to their deaths, to fight a hopeless defensive battle against the advancing Fritzes. It was typical of the pale-faced, cunning-eyed Chief-of-Staff: he would sacrifice anything and anybody for the Cause. Tomic hated and feared the man. Perhaps one day, if – Tomic dismissed his plans for future revenge and ventured, 'And what is the situation, Comrade General?'

Jovanovic looked up from the papers he was whipping through, obviously checking whether they were important enough to go with him. '*Situation?* Shit-awful . . . decidedly shit-awful. The Fritzes will take this place within the hour. We're down to perhaps a hundred men at the most, and those three Italian tanks we have are all knocked out. Those macaronis are no damn good with machines.'

'Where are we going?'

'To the First Proletarian Division. Two of its brigades are advancing on Drvar now. But they'll arrive too late. We'll meet them somewhere in the mountains and then we'll see.' He finished with the papers, tossed them in his waste-paper basket and dropped a lit match on top of them. 'Tito's column was ambushed,' he said, explaining his reason for summoning the chemist. 'We've not heard from them for over two hours now. It could well be we'll need you now, at last.'

Tomic gulped. For one fleeting moment, the enormity of his undertaking overcame him and he gasped, 'You really mean it, Comrade General?'

Jovanovic shrugged. 'Whatever happens now, we need you. *Le roi est mort, vive le roi.*'

'I'm sorry, I don't speak – er – Italian, comrade.'

'The king is dead, long live the king,' Jovanovic translated for him. 'Now come, pull that scarf up over your mug. They'll think you're trying to keep the stink of gunsmoke out. Let's go while we've still got time.'

Together the two plotters vanished through the door, leaving the papers in the basket burning like a funeral pyre.

'*Hurry, hurry, comrades!*' Tito urged repeatedly. Pistol in hand, he waved to the red-faced, panting men scrambling up the steep slope behind him. Most of them were half his age, yet the 52-year-old Marshal was much fitter. Tirelessly, he had led them ever higher during the past half-hour, setting a cracking pace which had them gasping for breath and lathering them in sweat within the first ten minutes. Twice they had bumped into little groups of German paratroopers, and both times the Marshal had been in the forefront of their attack, although the Lieutenant had protested fiercely. He had rushed them along with the rest of his men and personally shot one of the Fritzes who was trying to set up a machine-gun.

Tito was certain now that they were clear of the German paras; up here, he knew, the ground was too steep and rocky for a glider to land. Even though he believed they were safe from attack, he kept up the taxing pace.

His sole command was now a score or so of ragged, half-trained boys. He had to get back to the caves where his signallers and radios were located, to contact the English and ask for fighters and bombers to be sent from Italy to tackle the Fritzes. His own divisions and corps had to be given energetic direction. Jovanovic was able, but at this moment of extreme crisis he could not inspire the men like he, Tito, could.

Relentlessly, he urged his little body of men on, taking his bearings from the little compass he had strapped around his left wrist. He knew instinctively that the trail somewhere down below to his right would be blocked; however, the Fritzes obviously knew nothing about the caves to which this trail led. All the same, the Germans would continue to block it as one of the known exit routes from Drvar. Tito would have to make this detour through the mountains.

Time passed slowly as the small band of partisans frantically scrambled up and down steep slopes, clambering over huge boulders, clawing up shale walls, running bent-kneed down almost sheer inclines, with Tito not letting up on the pace for a moment. When a couple of the young men at the rear of the column, who were carrying the troop's heavy old-fashioned machine-gun, complete with tripod, groaned that they could not go on without a five-minutes break, Tito had levelled his pistol at them. Behind the gold-rimmed glasses his eyes were cold and heavy with menace. 'March or die,' he had said simply. They kept apace.

Now they were working their way along the edge of a heavy forest, which Tito seemed to recognize. He was sure that it was the one which fringed the mountain village. If that was the case, then they could not be more than a kilometre away from the caves. He changed direction, heading slightly south, taking them down from the mountains a little yet still avoiding getting too close to the trail, which he estimated lay beyond the low hills to his right. The going was easier now and the partisans' pace picked up. Tito smiled despite his nervousness and weariness. With luck they could not be much more than thirty-minutes march from the caves now. He forced himself to increase the pace, even though his wounds from the old war had begun to ache painfully.

Five minutes later he knew he had taken the right direction. On the next hilltop the familiar outline of Batasi came into view: a meagre collection of tumble-down cottages, clustered around the shabby church with its gleaming skate-roofed tower. He turned and forced a smile at his followers. 'We're nearly there—' he began.

In that same instant came the frightening roar of powerful engines. A silver shape came hurtling from the direction of the village, drawing its ominous black shadow across the houses behind it.

'Take cover!' the Lieutenant yelled.

The partisans flung themselves in all directions as the ME 109 came zooming in, its 20mm cannon blazing. Like a swarm of red-hot hornets, the tracers shells zapped towards them. Men screamed, as they exploded in their bodies, blasting them apart. Tito ducked behind a boulder, his head buried in the cold earth. A shell slammed into the stone and then he felt a hammer-blow against his head. Everything went black, and the great ear-splitting roar of the Messerschmidt as it dived and came in for another attack vanished ...

'Marshal Tito! ... Comrade!' the voice screamed in his ears. 'Comrade, *are you dead?'*

Tito blinked his eyes. A vague, blurred shape was bent over him. He blinked his eyes once more. The Lieutenant's face came into view, with tears running down his filthy face, tracing a white course through the dirt.

'No,' Tito said drily. 'I'm not dead – yet.'

'Thank God – thank God, for that!' the Lieutenant breathed, crossing himself in the Serbian fashion.

Tito ignored the movement, which seemed highly suspect for a communist officer. He struggled to his feet. The enemy plane was a faint speck on the horizon. But the Fritz had done his work well. Dead partisans were slumped everywhere; shattered bundles of bloody rags lying among the severed limbs. He shook his head to clear his ears of the ringing. 'How many men have you got left, Lieutenant?'

The officer did a swift count, wiping away his tears with his hand. 'Ten – no twelve, comrade.'

'They'll have to do!' Tito threw a glance at the village. Thick black smoke was pouring from the church tower, rising swiftly to the hard, still blue sky. It was a good sign. The Germans had shot up the village, too. That meant his own troops had not arrived yet. Still it was obvious that Germans were about. He would have to be careful. 'All right, let's go. But keep your eyes peeled, Lieutenant. There could be Fritzes about.'

The officer looked at him, naked admiration gleaming in his still wet eyes. 'Never fear, Comrade Marshal, every one of my men would lay down his life for you.'

Followed by the little band of survivors, Tito began to clamber down towards the trail.

The last stage of Marshal Tito's date with destiny had commenced.

The ME 109 came in in a graceful, slow curve. In the leading halftrack the troopers tensed. Had the pilot spotted the swastika flag stretched out across the bonnet for identification? He had and, crossing the column of Captain Attila's vehicle, he waggled his wings, then lowered his undercarriage to reduce his speed even more as he banked and came in once again.

Attila indicated to the driver he should stop, and waited, a puzzled frown on his lean, mutilated face.

One minute later his bewilderment had gone. A tiny parachute fell from the cockpit. He caught a glimpse of the white blur of the pilot's face, then the ME 109's undercarriage was up again and it was zooming away into the hard blue, leaving the parachute to fall gently to earth.

'Well, don't sit there like a spare prick at a wedding,' Attila snapped to his driver, '*Get it!*'

Hastily, Attila opened the little note scribbled in pencil. It read: *Report position to Gen. Rendulic – at once!* Then, below, the unknown pilot had added a hasty postcript: *Do you still love me?*

Attila grinned. Just like all the flyboys. Comics, the lot of them; they could afford to be. They were not down on the ground, getting their perfumed Air Force arses shot at.

'Operator,' he called, 'raise the big cheese – the General.'

Minutes later Rendulic himself was on the radio.

'Where in the three devils' name have you been *Hauptsturmführer?*' he raged. 'I've been waiting for you to call in for nearly an hour.'

'We had a little bit of bother,' Attila answered coolly, pausing to take a draw at his cheroot.

'What kind of bother?'

'A brigade of partisans moving south through the mountains,' Attila answered cheekily. 'Nothing much to speak about – we *only* took twenty dead and forty wounded.'

'Don't be so damned impertinent, *Hauptsturm*,' Rendulic snapped. 'Now report your position.'

'We're on some sort of forest trail heading south-east towards the village of Batasi.'

'Grid reference?'

Attila gave it, and there was a moment's silence at the other end while the General obviously checked out the reference on his map.

'Excellent, *Hauptsturm*. You're virtually dead on target.'

'And what is that, sir, if I may inquire?'

'The positions of Colonel Stuermer of Stormtroop Edelweiss.'

Attila frowned in bewilderment. For a minute the name and the unit meant nothing to him; then he recalled the tall, lean colonel of the High Alpine Corps with the cool, distant, blue eyes who had attended the Belgrade planning conference. 'You mean, General, that Colonel Stuermer has been behind the partisan lines all the time?' he exclaimed, losing his usual cynical reserve.

'Yes, for nearly four weeks to be exact, *Hauptsturm*.'

Attila whistled softly.

'You are to contact him and place yourself and your men at his command. Although you are of the SS, I have permission from *Reichsführer* Himmler himself for you to come under Colonel Stuermer's orders.'

'I see, sir,' Attila said woodenly, although he did not see at all. What the devil was this mysterious colonel, who had appeared out of nowhere, up to? 'May I ask what my mission is to be with Colonel Stuermer?'

There was a moment's hesitation at the other end, then Rendulic rasped, 'You may. You are to aid Colonel Stuermer in capturing Marshal Tito.'

Attila could not contain himself even though he knew he was talking to the Army Commander himself. '*Ouch, my aching arse!*' he exclaimed. '*Is that shittingly well all . . .?*'

FIVE

Stuermer could not see Drvar, but the pall of heavy black smoke which hung over the hills which surrounded it and the faint but distinct thump-thump of artillery which resounded in the still air told him that it was under severe attack. It was obvious that Operation Knight's Move was well underway after all.

Last night he had been about to give up. They had staked out the caves for nearly forty hours and their food was finished. On the previous evening all he had been able to offer his starving men had been a canteen of hot water, flavoured with a little sugar, two sweets, and a piece of mouldy sausage, all that could be looted from the bodies of the dead partisans at the glacier. The sight of his hungry young men turning the bread bags inside out in order to lick up whatever crumbs might still lie there had been too much for him. He had decided there and then to take them out if the attack did not materialize the following morning, even if it meant a court-martial for doing so. They had suffered enough in these last four weeks.

The morning's massive air raid and the following attack had changed all that. Immediately after it had started, he had called his men together and outlined his plan. Greul and his group would cover the northern approach to the caves; young *Leutenant* Hartmut the southern. As soon as it was dark, they would move in from each flank, cut off the caves from the village, while he, Ox-Jo and Jap and a handful of his most skilled climbers would come down from the roof of the caves by rope, hopefully taking the handful of sentries they had spotted the day before at the entrance by surprise. They seemed a careless bunch in their shirt-sleeves and without caps or weapons. Perhaps they were not even guards but just HQ staff.

THE STAKE-OUT, MAY 26th 1944

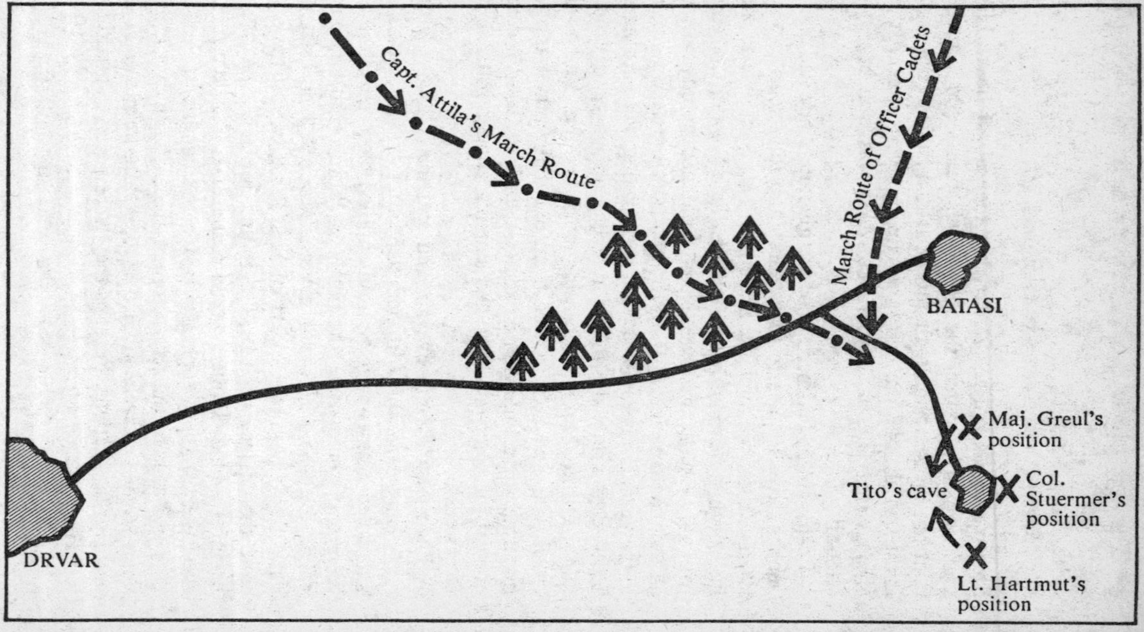

The men had listened attentively as he had outlined his plan, while the red rays of the dawn sun tinted their emaciated faces crimson.

When he was finished Ox-Jo had put his finger on the weak spot. 'Forgive my well-known dangling drawers, sir,' he had objected, 'but won't this lot of cock-eyed crookfingers—' he indicated the men all around him, squatting in the dust – 'probably hit *each other* in the darkness and not the Jugs? I mean, most of 'em usually miss the target – even when they charge it with fixed bayonet.'

Stuermer had chuckled and said, 'Could well be, Ox, but we're not going to do any firing once we're in those caves. None whatsoever.'

There had been several whistles of surprise and Ox-Jo had sneered, 'And what are we supposed to do if they don't exactly give us a knees-under-the-table sort of welcome, sir? *Tickle 'em to death!*'

'Not exactly, Ox. We'll use our bayonets, our entrenching tools, our bare hands if necessary. But not our bullets. We go in with our safeties on.'

Ox Jo had sighed. 'There's gonna be a lot of creamed drawers this night, I'll be bound,' he grumbled.

'Why waste good German lives on such rabble?' Greul had sneered. 'Kill the lot of them – it's the quickest and safest.

'I can't risk killing Tito in the process,' Stuermer had answered firmly. 'He must be taken alive.'

The briefing had taken place hours ago. All that morning they had waited, and most of the afternoon, too, but Tito had stubbornly refused to make his appearance from Drvar. Time after time Stuermer had searched the trail with his binoculars until his eyes ached, but there had been no sign of the missing Marshal.

Now it was late afternoon. His hungry, tense men had been in their positions for nearly ten hours, baking in the burning May sun. They lay concealed in the rocks and behind the boulders on both sides of the caves, not daring to move in case they caught the attention of the sloppy partisans lounging idly outside them. Would the damned Marshal never make his appearance?

Stuermer glanced at his watch yet again. It was nearly five. There'd be another two to two and a half hours of light. If the Marshal had not arrived by dusk, he would call the whole shitting operation off. His men must be fed and given a rest.

'Sir!' Cockeye hissed urgently.

'What?'

'They come!' Cockeye pointed a dirty finger in the direction of the trail and then ducked to avoid being seen from below.

Carefully, Stuermer crawled around the boulder behind which they hid and, shielding the glass of his binoculars lest the sun's rays catch it and betrayed his position, focused them.

A weary group of men, strung out in a long line, with the man bringing up the heavy machine-gun staggering along a hundred metres behind the rest, was coming down the hillside on to the trail.

He swept the line with his binoculars, counting them as he did so. They were partisans all right. Fourteen of them to be exact; young men all of them, save one who was much older and fatter; all of them were without badges of rank save the tallest, whom he thought was a lieutenant. Could this be Tito's party? Somehow he could not envision the partisan leader travelling with such a small escort. Besides, surely he would not move on foot, not such an important man!

Suddenly his ears were assailed by loud cries and then by cheers. He swung his binoculars around to the caves. The slovenly partisans standing at the entrances had been galvanized into excited action. They were springing up and down, waving their arms, swinging their weapons about delightedly. Obviously, they were greeting the new arrivals; he noticed them beginning to straighten up, pat their uniforms, button up collars while they continued to cheer.

'Same the whole world over,' Ox-Jo commented cynically, behind him. 'A big cheese is in the offing. Soldier boys begin filling their skivvies.'

Of course, Stuermer told himself urgently. This had to be Tito's party! Five minutes later his guess was confirmed. As the rest of the newcomers drew to one side, the portly, older man dressed in his nondescript uniform strode imperiously between the two lines of men standing rigidly to attention at the entrance to the caves. Stuermer caught one quick glimpse of his broad, powerful face, filled with ruthless energy, in spite of the genteel gold-rimmed glasses he wore, then Marshal Tito disappeared inside. They had him. *Tito had walked into the trap!*

He rolled over onto his back and glanced at Cockeye. 'All right, it's him,' he said quickly.

'Well, let's grab the sod and get out of here. My guts are doing back flips with hunger. I could eat a horse,' Ox-Jo growled.

'Yer, and that's probably what yer'll get when we get back to civilization. Nice, old giddi-up soup.'*

Stuermer smiled. All that an event of potentially historic importance meant to his two rogues was a chance to get something to eat. Yet perhaps they were right to view it that way. Then his smile vanished and he was businesslike again. 'Off you go to Major Greul and then over to Lieutenant Hartmut. Tell them our little bird has entered the trap. We go in one hour after darkness. Clear?'

'Clear, sir.' Cockeye slipped away noiselessly.

Stuermer sat down, and the little position behind the boulders drowsed in the hot sunshine, each man occupied with his own thoughts. In the distance, the battle at Drvar still raged, but Stuermer did not really hear it. Nor did he hear the heavy breathing of his companions. He felt abruptly unencumbered and strangely content. After all these weeks, they were finally going to end their mission. At that moment,

* Slang for horsemeat soup.

he told himself, he was like someone who had just made his will – his life ordered at last and the short road ahead clearly marked out.

There was nothing to do now but wait . . .

SIX

Attila ducked instinctively. Lead pattered like heavy tropical rain against the side of the half-track. Flinging up his arms with a soft groan, one of the troopers at the back pitched over the metal melodramatically. The second halftrack ran right over him, pressing his body into the dirt. As it drove on, one of the mangled trooper's arms waved as it rolled round and round with the suddenly bloody tracks, seeming to urge the men following to hurry.

The driver wanted to swing right, off the forest trail.

Angrily Attila slapped the hand holding the wheel. 'Keep going, damn you! Keep going! Or else—' His words were drowned out by another angry burst of machine-gun fire. He thanked his lucky stars that the partisans who were everywhere in the woods did not possess a German *panzerfaust.** On the steep narrow trail with no room to manoeuvre, they would have made short work of the German halftracks.

Ever since that last message from General Rendulic, the *Prinz Eugen* men had been passing through a large partisan formation. Attila's guess was that it must be at least a brigade, perhaps part of the 1st Proletarian Division, whose front he had broken that dawn. He was annoyed because they were slowing down his race to link up with Colonel Stuermer; although Attila had long had his fill of military honours – as he often told his cronies, 'I've got a desk-drawer full of tin, worth every bit of five marks' – he wanted to be in at the kill. After all, he had been seeking that damned Tito for nearly eighteen months now.

A hoarse, exultant scream cut through the air. Attila's heart sank. He knew what was coming – and it was worse than a damned *panzerfaust.* Multiple mortar filled the air frighteningly. The partisans had brought a captured German

* A kind of bazooka.

multiple mortar in action in an attempt to block the path of the advancing halftracks!

To his front the line of pines disappeared in a sudden cloud of grey smoke. Trees fell like match-sticks. Boughs flew through the air like severed limbs. A line of steaming brown holes barred his way.

Attila hardly had time to think what to do next when the mortar opened up again. Dark, red-tailed rockets hissed through the burning sky above the forest and landed directly on the two halftracks behind him. In an instant the shattered vehicles were filled with screaming dying men drowning in their own blood.

Attila reacted instinctively. '*Get that mortar!*' he screamed at the ashen-faced driver. '*Over there!*' He swung the wheel round himself and grabbed for his machine-pistol. '*Quick, for Chrissake!*'

The driver put his foot down hard. The big halftrack shot forward into the trees. Thick branches slapped at its metal sides as bushes were crushed under its whirling tracks. The crew of the mortar saw their danger. They dropped the rockets they were beginning to load and grabbed for their weapons. A man raised a grenade. Attila dropped him with a wild burst. The grenade fell to his feet and exploded under his dying body, sending him flying upwards; he came to rest in a bough ten metres up, like some grotesque bird roosting there.

At sixty kilometres an hour, the ten-ton halftrack slammed into the mortar and came to a sudden halt, rocking violently and spilling out its crew.

'*Out!*' Attila yelled over the hollow boom of metal striking metal.

His men needed no urging. They were out for blood after the day's events. With practised ease, they vaulted over the sides and ran at the partisans, guns blazing. The crew died where they lay. It wasn't war; it was murder. In the end, Attila had to slap the face of a wild-eyed boy who kept firing his machine-pistol into the bullet-riddled body of a partisan who was already dead. 'Save your shitting ammo, will you!' he screamed and, turning, took quick stock of his position.

The trail to his front was blocked. His rear was blocked, too. The two burning halftracks, filled with dead men, ensured that. He couldn't go backwards or forwards. At least, his vehicles could not, but the men could! Cupping his hands around his mouth, he bellowed above the crackle of small-arms fire, 'All right, you bunch of wet-tails, bale out! We'll do the rest on our big flat feet! Get the lead out of your wet britches!'

Five minutes later the surviving panzer grenadiers, with Attila jogging at their head, set off at the double.

Colonel Sevo, the one-armed head of the Officers' Training School, held up his hand. Behind him his hundred-odd officer-cadets came to a halt gratefully. They were superbly fit after the month's battle-school training, but the Colonel had set a cracking pace once he had heard that they were to come to the rescue of Tito himself and they were now glad to pause.

Sevo cocked his ear to one side. Yes, there it was again: the snap and pop of small arms fire to the west. It was not too far away, either. As the school's Chief-Instructor in Small Tactics, he had the ability to draw maps in his head. Now he mentally sketched in the details of the area from what he remembered from the last time he had seen the terrain on a map. The village would lie to the east, with the caves slightly south of that, located on the narrow side track. The firing coming from the west would indicate that the Fritzes were heading in the general direction of the caves. The Colonel licked suddenly dry lips. If the Fritzes managed to break off whatever action they were presently involved in and continued on their present route, they would be on a collision course with his command. Of one thing he was sure; they could have only one objective – Tito's cave.

Colonel Sevo was not a communist, but a soldier. As a

young man he had fought the Greeks and the Bulgarians; later, the Austrians and the Germans. He had lost his arm during the terrible retreat from Serbia under the old king, when only one out of every ten men of the beaten Serbian Army had survived. He had fought from the very start, of the present war, first with the Royal Army, later with the Chetniks, and then since 1942 with Tito. He knew the nature of war and he knew his duty. His responsibility was to Yugoslavia, and for him Tito, albeit a communist, represented the future of Yugoslavia. Therefore everything was to be sacrificed, if necessary, to save Tito.

Swinging round, undoing his own pack with difficulty, he faced his cadets. Blood-young, he could not help thinking, and damned red to boot, but patriots all the same. 'Gentle—' He caught himself abruptly and switched to the current form of address. 'Comrades, Tito is faced with danger, great danger. We must not think of ourselves. Even if we all die Yugoslavia must be saved. Get rid of all surplus equipment, packs, rations. Dead men don't need food.' He gave them an ancient grin, but it was not returned; they were dedicated, serious.

He waited until they stripped themselves of their surplus equipment – even their helmets, so that they stood there now strangely boyish with their long hair and armed solely with Tommy-guns and grenades. He cried, 'Now we run. Those who fall out *die*.' He pumped his one hand, fist clenched, up and down three times – the old infantry signal for at the double – and set off jogging. Behind him, his band of young men, already dedicated to death, followed.

It was going to be a race between the young grenadiers of the *Prinz Eugen* and the cadets. The collision course between the German and Slav elite troops had been set.

SEVEN

It was dark as Colonel Stuermer began carefully to lower the knotted rope. Next to him Ox-Jo, Jap and the handful of troopers he was taking with him slipped their socks on over the heavy mountain boots. There was no sound save the noise of the continuing battle from the direction of Drvar and the soft chatter of the two sentries at the entrance to the caves below.

'Here I go,' Stuermer whispered.

Taking the rope in both hands he went over the side of the rock-wall. The rope stretched taut under his weight. As gingerly as if he were walking on eggs, Colonel Stuermer braced his sock-covered boots against the rock to begin his descent. Hardly daring to breathe lest he alert the sentries, he descended with infinite slowness, feeling his way with his feet, endeavouring not to dislodge a single stone.

He knew from his survey of the rock-face by daylight that it was an easy descent; any amateur could have managed it without even raising a mild sweat. Under these conditions, however, it was damnably difficult, especially since just above the caves, there was an overhanging mantleshelf of rock where he would have to abandon the rope.

Millimetre by millimetre he descended as the chatter of the two sentries grew more audible. Now he could even smell the pungent odour of the English cigarettes they were smoking – obviously supplied in one of the para-drops made by the Tommies. Suddenly his covered boots struck rock. It was the mantleshelf. He tugged the rope three times, signalling Ox-Jo above to follow him, and then released his grip on it.

For a moment he balanced there precariously, praying he would not dislodge a stone now that he was only a matter of a dozen metres above the unsuspecting sentries' heads. Then he crouched and began to feel the rock for a handhold.

It took him a long time to find it. Not much of one – a shallow pocket hole – but it would have to do. He thrust his hand into it, tested it for stability and then swung his body out and downwards. For one long second, while his shoulder muscles screamed under the strain, he hung there, upside down, while his feet cautiously sought a grip. Then he corrected, breathing out a sigh of relief. Below all was silent: they had not heard him. He moved on. One minute passed, then another. He could not be more than a couple of metres above the entrance to the cave. In a minute he would have to play his little game with the two sentries.

Then his foot slipped! In a flash he found himself suspended, swinging frighteningly, connected to the rock-face only by his one hand tightly crammed into the hair-crack. How he held on, he never knew, he barely managed to suppress a scream of pain.

Gathering all his strength in tensing the muscles of his stomach and back, he thrust his lower body forward. His boots hit the rock, causing a soft thud, but they found no hold. He could hear the shuffle of the sentries' feet below. If they looked up now they'd see him hanging there in mid-air.

His shoulder muscles ablaze with searing pain, he breathed in deeply and tried again. His feet hit the rock-face and caught, giving him a hold! Trying not to move hastily but knowing he must relieve the almost unbearable strain on his shoulder muscles, he pressed down with his feet. The hold held. He relaxed his shoulder muscles gratefully, and for a long moment he did nothing more than wait for the much needed oxygen to be pumped into his bloodstream, while he rolled his shoulders systematically to ease both the pain and the strain. In a second, he knew, he would need to muster his strength and alertness, for he was now directly above and between the two sentries, who were silhouetted darkly against the expanse of night sky beyond.

'*Now!*' he commanded himself and dropped a pebble to their rear.

They started and spun round. In that same moment, he let go and dropped. The nearest one heard his fall and turned round. Stuermer's fist slammed into his stomach, sending him smashing back against the rockwall, all breath gone from him, his cry stifled by that terrible punch. Murmuring something in Serbian, in the darkness his comrade started to unsling his rifle with frantic fingers. Stuermer prevented him from completing the action.

Just as Ox-Jo's huge shape hurtled to the ground next to the partisan slammed against the rockwall, Stuermer rushed forward. He grabbed the man's helmet and pulled it down over his face, effectively blinding him and cutting off his cry of alarm. Stuermer's knee rammed cruelly into the sentry's stomach; again his howl of pain was muffled by the helmet clamped over his face. Stuermer kneed the sentry once more – and again. He felt rotten for doing it, but at least he was letting the sentry live, unlike Ox-Jo behind him, who was systematically bludgeoning the other fallen sentry to death with a home-made blackjack. Stuermer kneed the sentry for the third time. A sigh emitted from underneath the helmet and the man's sudden limpness told Stuermer that he had fainted. Gently, almost tenderly, he lowered him to the ground.

'Looks lovely, don't he, sir,' Ox-Jo whispered, obviously highly pleased with himself. 'Pleasant dreams, sonny-boy.' Grabbing the battered sentry with one hand and the unconscious one with the other, he dragged them out of the entrance, while Stuermer slipped behind the nearest rock-fold, where he would be concealed from anyone looking out from inside the cave.

Swiftly he pulled the bell-shaped signal-pistol from his belt and clicked off the safety. Raising it straight upwards, he pressed the trigger. A sharp click, a soft plop, and the green signal flare hissed into the night sky. It would tell the others waiting on the top of the caves to come down and would signal Greul and Hartmut that the Stuermer party was in position. For a moment the flare hung there, bathing the mountainside in its nasty green, unnatural light, casting a sickly hue on the faces of the two lone men staring up at it. Then it started to drop, allowing the darkness to creep back in again and conceal the horrors of this night.

'A green flare!' the Colonel gasped to himself, not pausing for an instant. 'Fritz!'

He had seen their type of signal flares in two wars and knew what green signified. *Grün ist die Hoffnung*,* they said in their barbaric tongue. It was the colour of success. Obviously they had cut the track to the cave and they were in position. To do what?

There was no time to answer that frightening question. All he knew was that the flare signified trouble. 'Prepare for trouble,' he called back, still not slackening his pace.

Behind him he could hear the sweat-lathered, gasping young officer-cadets unslinging their weapons and snapping off the safeties. Grimly, he pulled out his own pistol with his one hand and did the same, but with more difficulty.

Waving his pistol, he yelled 'Follow me! ... There is no time to be lost!'

The cadets, eager for some desperate glory and filled with the crazy youthful desire to sacrifice themselves, plunged on through the trees.

Hauptsturmführer Attila, too, saw the green flare as it curved into the night sky, some half a kilometre away. Instinctively, he knew that it must be Stuermer. He knew from Rendulic there were no other German troops in the area. His heart leapt and even his habitual cynicism vanished for a moment. Green for success. Did the flare mean that the Alpine Corps Colonel had captured Tito?

But why was there no firing – no sound of any kind of action whatsoever? The Jugs would not have let their leader

* Green is hope.

simply be captured, without offering any kind of resistance, he reasoned. Did the green flare only signify that Stuermer had successfully got into position for an attack?

Suddenly his ears were assailed by the myriad, minute sounds a large body of men cause when they are making their way hastily through a forest – the clink of equipment, metal against metal, the snap and crack of branches underfoot, the little angry cries of men slipping on wet leaves and banging into tree trunks in the inky darkness.

They could not be German!

He hissed an urgent warning to his panting grenadiers. They dropped in their tracks, weapons at the ready, trying to calm the sudden urgent thumping of their hearts as they peered into the night, waiting.

Colonel Sevo's cadets were running right into a trap!

EIGHT

Carefully the troopers worked their way down the entrance, keeping to the shadows. The faint hum of radios and subdued sound of voices further up ahead indicated that the partisans were perhaps fifty or sixty metres away.

Nerves tingling expectantly, Stuermer took stock of his surroundings. The cave was a natural one, but it had been worked upon. Its roof had been chiselled straight to allow for the wires which ran its length to the placed into position; in the light of the two blue-painted, naked bulbs which hung there, he could see that the floor had been smoothed and covered with duck-boards.

In spite of the faint voices and the evidence of human hands, there was something eerie and threatening about the entrance's very emptiness. Stuermer fought the desire to turn back and clear off with his handful of men while there was still time. Controlling himself, he continued his infinitely slow progress forward.

The partisans must be taken by complete surprise. His men were well disciplined; they would not fire. But the partisans might fire, if they had a chance, and in the confined space of the caves, a richocheted bullet might put an end to the life of the man they had come so far to capture. He told himself that they must prevent that at all costs, whatever risks Stormtroop Edelweiss might run in the process.

The minutes ticked by. They passed a side-cave, its door covered by a thick felt blanket, and heard heavy snores coming from behind it. Stuermer gave a signal to Jap. The little half-breed stole forward, a wicked-looking, curved knife clasped in his surprisingly small yellow paw. He brushed aside the curtain noiselessly and disappeared. For a long moment nothing happened. Then came the sudden squeak of bed-springs and a hushed, sharp, abruptly stifled gasp, like that – Stuermer thought with an absurd memory of other times – of a woman in the moment of climax. Seconds later, Jap reappeared, wiping the blood of the slaughtered men on the felt blanket. He nodded at the Colonel.

They padded on. Another side cave. But it was empty save for a pile of equipment, rifles, and what looked like a straw bed of the kind one might make for a watch-dog. Stuermer jerked his head at the nearest trooper. He knew what to do without being told. Entrenching tool held at the ready, he stood guard over the rifles. No wandering partisans were going to get their hands on them when the balloon went up.

The voices from within were becoming much clearer, and the tense little group of troopers creeping down the ill-lit corridor could hear the buzz of morse quite distinctly. Suddenly Stuermer froze. Further up the gloom of the cave, he could hear a soft pad-padding, and his nostrils were suddenly assailed by the raunchy smell of dog.

'Shit!' Ox-Jo exclaimed behind him. 'Watch-dog!'

A big yellow-brown Alsatian appeared around the bend and stopped, sniffing the air, its lips drawn back slightly to reveal large yellow teeth and foam dripping at both sides of long, wolfish jaw.

Stuermer swallowed hard as he watched its ears go flat, its lean muscular body push back a little on the powerful hind-legs its upper lip wrinkle upwards to reveal menacing teeth. He knew the signs: in one moment the dog would spring.

A low growl started deep down inside Tiggan's throat as it sank even lower on its haunches.

'*No noise!*' Stuermer hissed, tensing. 'We can't—'

The words died on his lips as the dog sprang in the same moment that Ox-Jo threw himself in front of his beloved CO. One hundred pounds of muscle and flesh hit him. In spite of his massive bulk, Ox went down on his knees, suddenly submerged in fur and the stench of animal. The dog's claw raked his cheek, and blood started to pour down his face. The scent of blood turned Tiggan crazy. Its teeth shot for Ox-Jo's throat. The big mountaineer threw up his right hand just in time. He swallowed a yelp of agony as the animal's teeth crunched into his fingers. Desperately, he shot up his other hand. Luck was on his side. He found and clenched the alsatian's snout.

Crazily Tiggan tried to free itself. With its back legs it tore furiously at Ox-Jo's chest, ripping his jacket and shirt to shreds with its razor-sharp claws, gouging out deep chunks of flesh, levering deep bloody scratches the whole length of his hairy breast. With all his strength Ox-Jo held on, while the others watched this strange, silent battle on the floor in impotent anxiety. Madly, the choking dog squirmed back and forth, trying to free itself from that iron grip. Bleeding heavily, sweating and panting with the effort of trying to hold on to the dog, Ox-Jo exerted all his energy to maintain his grip.

Suddenly the dog flexed all its muscles and flung itself to one side. The trick caught Ox-Jo completely off guard. The dog took a great breath and then springing to its feet, rushed at Ox-Jo's throat, heading in for the kill, while Ox-Jo lay sprawled, completely defenceless.

Tiggan never reached that naked, bared throat. Jap threw himself on top of the animal, his knife flashing. Once ... twice . . . three times, in and out, its blade reddening. Tiggan, loyal to the end, fought back, getting weaker but not even whimpering with the tremendous pain that racked its body. Suddenly it went limp and flopped on one side, its chest racked by shallow gasping convulsions. Panting, Jap with his knife upraised watched it suspiciously, but Tiggan's eyes soon turned upwards at the same moment that its jaw dropped. The dog was dead.

Nobody moved. The whole scene seemed frozen, as if for ever: Jap with the upraised, dripping-red knife; Ox-Jo sprawled, blood-stained and torn about the face, next to the dead dog; and the rest staring down at them, eyes filled with horror.

Stuermer broke the tension by reaching down and taking Ox-Jo's bleeding hand. 'Up,' he whispered. 'Come on you big rogue.'

Two minutes later they reached the door, behind which came the hum of many radios, voices, and the staccato chatter of morse. They had reached their objective. Behind the door was the man they had come so far to capture.

Stuermer licked his lips, hesitating. The next few moments would be decisive. The fate of Germany might well depend on what would happen. Then he nudged Jap and his lips formed the word *now.*

Jap slipped his knife in his belt and took out the smoke bomb, a last minute idea on Stuermer's part. All around him the others tensed. They all knew what was going to happen: the little half-breed would open the door and toss in the bomb; when it exploded they would go in, wielding their clubs, while Ox-Jo and Jap guarded the door behind them against intruders.

Jap shot an inquiring glance at the others. Knowing what it meant, they slipped on the damp handkerchieves which were going to serve them as primitive smoke masks. He nodded and tugged the pin out of the round bomb. The fuse started to splutter furiously. The others, only their anxious eyes revealed now above the wet clothes, watched as he counted out the seconds.

One ... two ... three ... four! With a sudden burst of energy, he grasped the door handle and turned it.

The door was locked from the inside!

NINE

At the same moment that Jap tried the door and found it locked, some five hundred metres away in the darkness outside Colonel Sevo's cadets ran straight into the ambush prepared for them by Attila's panzer grenadiers.

They were stopped as if they had walked right into a brick wall. They went down everywhere, threshing about the undergrowth in their agony, caught completely off guard by the scarlet stabs that cut the night on all sides.

Sevo went down, pulled off his feet by a screaming cadet whose arm had been ripped off by a vicious salvo of machine-gun fire. He fell among the writhing bodies, hearing their gruesome bellows as they were wounded again. For a second he lay there, pistol gone, feeling the tracer zip hotly across his prostrate body; he did not want to get up again and face that murderous fire, but he hold himself he had to.

He turned and scuttled across a soft carpet of writhing bodies, the night made hideous by their screams as they called for help that would never come. He tripped and fell, finding his face buried in a huge bloody hole. Wiping away the gore with his one hand, he carried on.

Outlined clearly now by the trees which had begun to burn to their right, he could see a small rise. It would have to do. He'd rally what was left of his cadets there. Pushing his boots cruelly into the soft body of a dying cadet, he dived forward. A moment later he was behind the cover of the hillock, and the bullets which had followed him were thudding purposelessly into the earth at the other side.

He rested there briefly, gathering strength, his chest heaving frantically; then he sprang to the top of the hillock, clearly outlined by the stab and flash of small arms fire all around him.

'This is Colonel Sevo!' he bellowed above the racket.

'Your Colonel. Cadets, rally on me!'

Immediately the German fire concentrated on the lone one-armed figure who stood swaying on the rise. But he seemed to bear a charmed life. The bullets whipped and tugged at his uniform, stitching countless holes in it but missing his body.

The sight of him, the old man, standing there, bareheaded and unarmed yet defying the German fire all by himself, had the effect Sevo thought it would. Wounded and unwounded alike rose from the ground and with all their strength ran to the Colonel. Here and there a seriously wounded man hobbled or even crawled after them, whimpering piteously, begging not to be left behind.

The German machine-gunners turned their attention on the fleeing men, but they had been caught off guard. By the time the first bursts had started felling the laggards, fifty-odd cadets had dived over the hillock, tugging their Colonel down with them, and were beginning to return the German fire. They shot wildly at first, but under the Colonel's direction their aim swiftly became more accurate.

Fifty metres away, *Hauptsturmführer* Attila spat away the stump of his unlit cheroot in disgust and cursed. Thanks to that one-armed devil, his ambush had not paid off the dividends he had expected. Now both sides were bogged down. The bloody slogging match had commenced.

It looked as if he would damn well not be in at the kill after all.

For one long moment the men in the large underground room lit by the poor light of the electric bulbs stared at each other in shock. The muted but definite fire-fight outside and the noise at the locked door made it quite clear what was happening. The Fritzes were already there! Even the ever resourceful Tito, who had been in many desperate situations during his long underground life, was shocked into inactivity. It was the tall youthful lieutenant who had accompanied him from Drvar who acted first.

'Cover the door with the machine-gun!' he cried at his dazed men. 'Move, will you!'

He grabbed hold of the man holding the English Bren and thrust him forward. The man shook his head, as if he were waking from a deep sleep, and then dropped on his knees to set up his automatic. His number two fell down beside him and clipped on the magazine.

'The rest of you,' the Lieutenant commanded, 'form a firing line! You operators—' he whirled round at the pale-faced men of the HQ staff – 'with me!'

Not waiting for them to follow, he doubled forward into the darker interior of the cave where, he knew, the air shaft lay. 'Each of you grab a crate,' he bellowed and started pushing crates together furiously, underneath the air shaft which was some twelve metres above him. '*Quick!*'

Outside there was an ominous silence, but he knew it could be only a matter of minutes before the Fritzes came bursting in, guns blazing. The Marshal had to be out by then. Leaving his radio operators to continue the job of building the improvised stairs, he grabbed Tito by the arm. 'Marshal, you must go. *Please!*'

Outside the silence was shattered by the sound of rifle-butts hammering harshly at the door, which was already starting to splinter under the blows.

Tito hesitated.

'Please Marshal, I shall accompany you,' the Lieutenant urged frantically. 'You, comrades, you must hold them back. Even if you have to die to do so. Give us five minutes. *Just five!* Now Marshal, *come!*'

He could wait no longer. The upper panel of the door was already smashed through. A yellow hand was feeling through the splintered wood, obviously looking for the key.

On the floor the gunner pressed the trigger. The Bren gun chattered into action, ripping holes all along the wood. There was a scream and the sound of someone falling heavily.

A bomb came hurtling through the hole and exploded with a soft plop. Next instant thick white choking smoke started to stream from it. Coughing and spluttering, tears stinging his eyes, the young officer pushed a choking Tito in front of him and helped him up on to the first crate. Together they scrambled up the precariously swaying stairs. Their breathing grew easier as they climbed above the white cloud of smoke below, which now nearly obscured the chaos of the inner cave. In the same moment that the door finally shattered and the Germans came storming into the room to be met by a hail of wild fire, the two men disappeared into the air shaft.

Stuermer kicked aside a body that sprawled in his path, the wound in his shoulder burning like fire. Feeling two hands grasp his jacket, he kneed the unseen partisan instinctively. Bellowing in pain, whoever had grabbed him fell back into the smoke-filled confusion.

Stuermer trampled over the dead and wounded lying everywhere between the radios, his boots digging deep into the carpet of their bodies. His foot caught somewhere, sending him sprawling full-length. A face loomed up in front of him. Bearded. A partisan. He slammed his fist into it blindly, forcing it back.

'Clear out this shitting smoke!' Ox-Jo was bellowing, defending himself like a wild beast against the partisans who were all around him, lashing out with boot and fist.

There was no room for the partisans to fire their weapons. Now it was every man for himself. Entrenching tools, clubs, knives flashed, slashed, smashed, ripped, gouged, chopped. German and Slav rolled and writhed together among the dead, hands locked on each other's throats to the bitter end, even in their dying agonies.

But help was on the way. As Stuermer struggled with a big partisan who had a gory pit where his right eye should have been, there was the sound of heavy boots running from the entrance and harsh cries in German. It was Greul and his group! With all his remaining strength and sobbing with the effort, Stuermer thrust his finger straight into the ghastly wound. The partisan screamed hideously. Then his spine arched taut like a bow string – and he fell back dead.

The shouts died away into groans. The groans gave way to whimpers and hopeless sobs. The smoke started to clear as Greul's men began to herd the surviving partisans against the wall. Stuermer, his body racked with pain, his breath coming in short hectic gasps, surveyed them, accompanied by Greul and Ox-Jo, who hopped on one leg while blood streamed down the naked calf of the other one.

The partisans were all young. Tito was not among them. Wordlessly, the German troopers started to check the dead, turning over the bodies littering the floor. Tito was not there either.

Greul lost his patience. He strode up to the nearest partisan, a handsome boy with blood trickling down his pale face from a wound in his temple. 'Where is Tito?' he demanded. When the boy did not answer, he smashed his fist in rage into the boy's face, sending him reeling against the wall.

'Stop that!' Stuermer shouted. He had already seen the direction of the boy's gaze and what lay there – the pile of crates. 'Come on!'

Forgetting his wound, he bounded across the cave, smashing through a knot of his own men, followed by Greul and a limping Ox-Jo. He skidded to a halt and squinted upwards at the dark air shaft. Some forty or fifty metres above, he could just make out a lighter patch. The exit.

'Come on!' he said. 'Follow me! That's the way he went!'

TEN

The Lieutenant tensed. His courage was running out; he knew it would not last much longer. He could not run nor fight any more. His energy was spent.

'They're coming up,' Tito said tensely, saying aloud what he already knew. His keener ears had caught the sound of their nailed boots on the first rungs of the air shaft seconds before. 'They'll find us here.'

'No, they won't, Comrade Marshal,' the Lieutenant forced himself to say, taking out his pistol and placing it on the rock next to his last grenade. 'At least not *you.*'

'What—'

'You see over there – ' the Lieutenant said, interrupting him urgently, indicating the tracer which sailed through the darkness like fireflies. 'Our men are out there somewhere. You must reach them.'

'And you?'

'I shall stay here and hold them back.'

'But—'

'There are no buts, Comrade Marshal. Who am I? A nobody. Your life is worth a thousand insignificant existences such as mine. Before the war I was a book-keeper in a shoe factory. If I survive it – 'he corrected himself – 'if I did survive it, I would return to being a book-keeper once again. But you are the future. You are Jugoslavia.' He stuck out his dirty hand. 'Good-bye, comrade!'

Tito took the Lieutenant's hand and pressed it hard, tears stinging his eyes. 'Good-bye, comrade!' he said fervently, hearing the footsteps on the iron rungs getting ever louder. The Germans would be on the top of the shaft in seconds. 'Give me a minute – and then surrender, do you understand?'

'I understand, comrade,' the Lieutenant said, knowing as he said the words that there was no surrender.

Then Tito was running into the night, leaving the Lieutenant tensed opposite the exit, pistol in hand.

When Greul stuck his head out of the shaft, the Lieutenant pressed the trigger. Scarlet flame spurted from his pistol. Greul screamed with pain and reeled back, plummeting past a shocked Stuermer and then smashing to the bottom of the shaft, where he lay sprawled among the shattered crates, his leg tucked under his body at an unnatural angle.

The Colonel had no time to concern himself with the fate of his second-in-command. His ears had already caught the noisy spluttering of a grenade coming his way. If it fell into the shaft, packed now with his troopers, it would create terrible havoc. Almost unconsciously he thrust up his good arm above the hole. Something metallic slapped into it, as if by a miracle. The grenade!

He flung it back blindly. In the same moment that it exploded in a burst of flame, sending the young Lieutenant reeling back screaming, blinded and minus both hands, Stuermer hurled himself up and out. In a flash he was on his feet and running, followed by a handful of troopers, seeing now the full blast of the battle going on ahead. He sprang over the body of the dying Lieutenant. Up on a ridge to the right, he could see a portly figure running, clearly outlined by the flashes of the battle. It had to be Tito.

'*Stehenbleiben!*' he yelled and fired a swift burst way above the fugitive's head to frighten him into halting.

The slugs whined off the boulders to Tito's right, sending fear hooting through his bowels, but he kept on running. He could not be more than a hundred metres from the thick of battle. Once there, he'd be safe.

Stuermer cursed and cried to his men, 'All right, swing out on both sides and try to stop him – and in three devils' name, don't fire. I want him alive!'

Tito, his heart thumping crazily, ran with all his remaining strength. The slugs from the battle ahead whistled all around him, but he knew they were harmless, richochets for the most part. Behind him, he guessed, his pursuers must have known that, too, for they did not stop now they had entered the danger zone; they kept on coming.

Tito, cursed, wondering which was his own side. He zigzagged to right and then to left, trying to pick up his bearings in the confused fire-fight that was taking place among the pines, straining his ears in an attempt to identify weapons which were used only by the partisans. But it was damnably difficult; both sides were employing weapons captured from each other.

Then he heard the slow chatter of a Bren-gun, the English automatic rifle used only by the partisans because the Fritzes did not have the 303 ammunition it needed. He changed direction hastily. His pursuers were now only a matter of metres away, but he would beat them yet. Suddenly his mind was full of the use he would make of this last-minute rescue. It might well be a way of rallying his obviously disorganized divisions. If he, an aged Marshal, could save himself from the Fritzes, then surely his well-trained youthful divisions could? *Agitprop* would be able to make a splendid propaganda out of their success.

With all his remaining strength, he doubled forward towards the sound of the Bren, crying in Serbian, 'Don't shoot! ... Don't shoot! ... I'm Tito! ... *TITO!*'

Lying in his shallow pit, blood pouring from his head, where the dead partisan sprawled next to him had knifed him, his trousers filled with the faeces of fear, nauseated and sick at heart, the lone seventeen-year-old fired the Bren aimlessly at the shadows. He knew he had to do something or he would begin screaming uncontrollably with terror. Then he stared at the dark figure running towards him.

The young German trooper had been cut off from the rest of the *Prinz Eugen* for over a quarter of an hour now, though it had seemed an eternity. When the bearded partisan had jumped him, he had dropped his rifle, overcome with fear, his bowels evacuating themselves sickeningly. The partisan had laughed in triumph, dropping his Bren and raising the knife he carried in his other hand. Abruptly the youth had recalled the bodies of comrades he had seen the previous month after they had been captured by the partisans – their genitals gouged out, their members then placed between their dead lips in mockery. He had rolled over desperately as the knife had flashed down. Somehow his hands had found the partisan's throat and somehow he had managed to strangle the life out of him, tears of terror streaming down his youthful face.

Now this new figure was running for him, arms upraised. Was is one of his own comrades. '*Prinz Eugen?*' he called hesitantly.

There was no reply. The man came on, shouting something unintelligible.

'*Prinz Eugen?*' he called louder.

'*Tito ... Tito ...*'

The youth's finger curled around the trigger of the Bren. The man was shouting '*Tito*'. He was one of them! To his right a flare exploded. It coloured the running man a frightening blood-red, showing the terrified youth every detail of his figure.

A hundred metres away a shocked Stuermer could see them, too: the battle-littered ground, the dead, the running figure and the boy in the camouflaged outfit of the SS crouched behind the machine-gun. 'Don't shoot!' he cried desperately, running full-tilt with the last of his strength to stop the tragedy. '*For God's sake, don't shoot!*'

The flare went out. For a moment Stuermer was blinded by the sudden pitch-darkness. He was forced to stop; he could not see anything. He blinked his eyes and regained his vision, then began to run again. But not for long. A sudden chatter of the Bren exploded to his right and he knew instinctively it was too late. He stopped running and leaned against a tree, its bullet-severed branches lying on the ground all around like sawn-off limbs. Colonel Stuermer his shoulders sag in defeat.

Tito was dead!

Dawn. A heavy silence lay over the battlefield, broken only by the whimpering of the wounded as the orderlies in their blood-stained aprons probed their wounds.

Wearily, Stuermer stamped over the area, ignoring the dead everywhere, searching the ground. The boy with the Bren trotted after him, his dirty, tear-stained face contorted in fear and pride.

Stuermer stopped. 'Was it here?' he demanded, overcome by a great tiredness.

'I think so,' the boy began. 'Yes . . . yes, it was here. There's the Jug I killed last night. With my bare hands,' he added, gaining confidence. After all, the Captain had promised him the Iron Cross, First Class for last night's work.

'Well, where's his body?'

'They must have taken it with them – the partisans, when they pulled back last night after your people arrived, Colonel.'

Colonel Stuermer grunted non-committally.

'But I caught him with a full burst at ten metres' range, sir!' the boy protested, seeing the Iron Cross and the fourteen days' leave in the Homeland which Captain Attila had promised him vanishing before his eyes. 'He couldn't have survived that. Nobody could, sir.'

Again Stuermer grunted. With difficulty due to his wounded arm, roughly bound in a provisional sling, he bent down and touched the grass with his fingers. They came away red. Blood! But was it that of the Marshal?

'Look here, sir!' the boy said with sudden excitement. 'Look what I've found.'

Stuermer straightened up slowly. The boy, his face flushed triumphantly, was holding up a pair of gold-rimmed spectacles, with one lens completely smashed, as if by a bullet. 'Didn't you say he wore gold-rimmed glasses, sir?' he asked.

'I did.'

Stuermer took them out of his hand and examined them carefully in the grey, unreal light of the new dawn. During his last glimpse of the missing partisan leader, just before the red flare had dropped and gone out, he had seen the glasses gleaming an eerie blood-red in that ghastly glare: glasses just like these which he now held in his hand.

For a long time Stuermer stood among the stiff bodies of the dead, staring down at the glasses, trying to make up his mind. Had Tito really been killed by the burst? Was it only a dead body that the officer-cadets had been able to drag away with them before they had disappeared into the mountains? Or had Tito managed to crawl away under his own steam?

Hauptsturmführer Attila's cynical voice disturbed the heavy silence. 'I'm afraid there'll be no tin collar in this one for either of us, Colonel Stuermer.' He chuckled maliciously. 'You know what they say – no body, no payee!'

Stuermer awoke from his reverie. He smiled weakly and handed the glasses back to the boy. 'You're right there, *Hauptsturm.* No body, no payee.' His voice hardened. 'Come on, let's get out of this damned place, once and for all. I've had a noseful of it!'

Together they walked back to the trucks waiting to take them out of the mountains. Behind them the boy dogged their heels, holding the precious spectacles, which were his proof of his great deed. 'I'll keep them for ever,' he was promising himself at that moment. 'As a souvenir for my kids when I have them.' He grinned at thought of how those kids would be made. 'For ever!' And he did – until he was shot in an ambush two months later and the partisan who looted the dead youth's kit threw them away in disgust because he found neither food nor money in the Fritz's pack.

Slowly the trucks started to draw away, heading west, leaving the silent mountains to the dead . . .

POSTSCRIPT

'*Impossible!*' Greul snorted, as Lieutenant Hartmut, clad like the rest of them on the sunny hospital terrace in the blue-and-white striped pyjamas of the wounded, read the caption in his hesitant English.

'What does it say, sir?' Jap asked, leaning on his cane.

Hartmut translated. '*Marshall Tito arriving at the harbour of Komisa . . . on the island of Vis . . . to take command of his Army again after his successful escape from Hun* – that's us,' Hartmut explainted in an aside – '*trap in mountains . . .*'

Colonel Stuermer squinted against the sun's glare and stared at the picture: Tito, dressed in a resplendent uniform, surrounded by grinning Tommy sailors on the deck of what looked like a destroyer. Next to him, an alsatian squatted on its haunches patiently, its long tongue hanging out of its open jaws, as if it were very hot on the deck.

The memory of that other dog flashed through Stuermer's mind abruptly. That one and the one in the picture were identical, as far as he could make out. But so was its owner. Had they killed Tito or had they not?

In the month since they had returned from the mountains for treatment in this peaceful Bavarian hospital not far from Berchtesgaden under the general supervision of Hitler's own doctor Professor Morrell, Stuermer had begun to think that the whole Jugoslavian operation had been a dream. Had they really made that long trek through the mountains, fought so many dangers, entered those caves and shot it out with the partisans? Had he really seen Tito fleeing straight into the bullets of the machine-gun held by that stinking, frightened boy? His wound told him he had, yet it was hard to believe.

The Führer had sent a personal telegram of congratulations. Admittedly they had not captured the elusive partisan leader, but the partisan army was in 'complete disarray', fleeing through the mountains, 'a broken force'; the situation in the Balkans had 'been saved, at least, for the time being'. But what of Tito? Nothing had been heard of him from either friendly or enemy sources until the appearance of this English paper, the *News Herald*, which the despatch rider had brought up with the rest of their mail from the High Alpine Corps HQ this fine June morning.

There he was, as large as life, smiling somewhat coldly and uncertainty, but smiling all the same at the grinning Tommy sailors, a mild twinkle in the dark eyes behind the gold-rimmed spectacles. There was no denying it. There in the poor quality picture was the man they thought they had killed one month before, Marshal Tito!

'A double,' Ox-Jo growled, slapping the thick plaster cast that still surrounded his wooden leg as if to emphasize his point. 'They all have doubles, those big cheeses. That Jug is a double.'

Greul looked at him. 'The Führer doesn't have a double, Sergeant-Major,' he said coldly.

Ox-Jo raised one haunch and farted contemptuously. '*Heil Hitler!*' he said.

Greul flushed and opened his mouth, but before he could speak, the dust-covered despatch-rider who had brought the mail up from the valley said, 'I wonder if the senior officer would sign for the Blitz, please, gentlemen?' He looked at their pyjama-clad shapes a little puzzled, for they bore no badges of rank.

'The Blitz?' Stuermer asked.

The despatch-rider indicated the buff-covered telegram envelope, which bore the eagle stamp and the usual legend *Geheime Reichssache.**

'Yes, hand me your pad, my man,' Ox-Jo said grandly. Before anyone could stop him, he had signed it with a flourish.

The despatch-rider looked down at the signature, then clicked to attention. 'Thank you, Colonel,' he snapped and saluted.

* Roughly, 'top secret.'

Ox-Jo gave him a casual senior officer's salute. 'Now then, be off with you, my man. And watch those bends in the road. They're dangerous.'

'Thank you, sir. Yes, I will, sir,. Good-bye, sir.' The despatch-rider backed away towards his motorbike, as if he were in the presence of royalty. While Greul glared, Stuermer shook his head, 'Ox, one day the Army's going to take you – and hang, draw and quarter you, *slowly*!'

'That'll be the day,' Ox-Jo said, in no way disconcerted, eyeing the plump backside of one of the nurses, who was bending over another patient on the terrace and revealing a delightful expanse of thigh.

Slowly Stuermer opened the top-secret cable while Greul and Hartmut stared at him curiously. 'It's from *Reichsführer* Himmler,' he announced.

Greul's face lit up. 'What does he say, sir?' he asked eagerly, knowing that anything the fanatical head of the SS had to say must mean action for Stormtroop Edelweiss sooner or later. With the Anglo-Americans already landed in Normandy, he, Greul, did not want to waste any more time in hospital when his Fatherland was in danger.

Stuermer cleared his throat. '*Tito Mark Two performing well, as you can see from enemy periodicals . . . All the same, congratulations to you and your brave men. Herewith I admit Stormtroop Edelweiss to the Armed SS*,' Stuermer bit his bottom lip.

Greul's light blue eyes blazed fanatically. '*The Armed SS!*' he breathed ecstactically. 'What an honour!'

'Could be dangerous,' Ox-Jo commented, not taking his eyes off the nurse's delightfully creamy thighs and telling himself with a soft stirring of desire he'd sacrifice a bit of his salami for her any day.

'There's more,' Stuermer said, recovering from the shock that now he was a colonel in the Black Guards, a high-ranking member of that vulgar, cruel hierarchy which had caused so much misery in Germany and abroad.

'Give us it, please, *Obersturmbannführer*,' Greul beamed

at Stuermer as he used his new Armed SS rank-designation.

Wearily, Stuermer complied. '*Best wishes for a speedy recovery. Need Edelweiss urgently for Operation Stalin Gold . . . Heil Hitler . . . Signed Himmler . . .*'

'*Operation Stalin Gold!*' the others breathed. 'What's that?'

Instinctively, Stuermer knew. They were pulling out of Russia after the three years of bloody slaughter which had decimated Germany's armies, taking their loot with them. The rats were leaving the sinking ship, and he and his men were going to do their dirty work for them.

Miserably, he let the Blitz flutter down to the floor in the same moment that a delighted Ox-Jo caught a brief glimpse of crisp black curly hair which indicated the nurse was not a true blonde and that she had decided not to put on an essential part of her clothing on this burningly hot morning. He turned and beamed at the solemn-faced Stormtroop men all around him on the bright, white terrace. 'Things are looking up, aren't they?' he exclaimed. 'Yes, these days, every morning brings a new surprise . . .'

MOUNTAIN OF SKULLS

Leo Kessler

The Black Cossacks had burned, looted, raped, slaughtered their way across half Europe – from the frozen wastes of Russia to the mountains of northern Italy – as soldiers of Hitler's Reich.

Now it was the spring of 1945 and the Fuhrer's shattered armies were reeling back on every front. But for the Cossacks there could be no surrender. Peace meant Stalin's revenge and death for everyone of them. So it was that as Germany retreated General Alexei Bogdan led his Russian warrior elite once more, against all odds, into the attack.

Also available in this series:

THE BLACK COSSACKS
SABRES OF THE REICH

WORLD WAR II

James Jones

A unique account of the Second World War – a personal front line narrative by a GI who became one of the most popular authors of our time with his million-selling novel FROM HERE TO ETERNITY. Alternately moving and humorous, WWII is also a brilliant history of the war as a whole, illustrated with original eyewitness paintings by soldiers from both sides.

'There may be more comprehensive illustrated histories of the war but none is likely to come closer than WWII to conveying the feeling of how it was to be there'. *Time Magazine*

'Outstanding . . .' *Sunday Telegraph*

'A blockbuster of a book' *Financial Times*